Thunder Road
Goodyear, God & Gatorade

By
Tom McAuliffe

NEXT STOP PARADISE
PUBLISHING
Ft. Walton Beach, Florida, USA

Thunder Road
Goodyear, God & Gatorade

by Tom McAuliffe

Book ISBN #979-8-9892712-8-3

First EDITION - 2024

For more information email:
bookinfo@nextstopparadise.com

WWW.AUTHORTOMMCAULIFFE.COM

<u>Dedications</u>

To the Men, Women and Fans of NASCAR

For anyone that has ever had their head
under a hood or their foot to the floor!

**100% of the profits of this book will be
donated to The NASCAR Foundation.**
https://www.nascarfoundation.org/

TABLE OF CONTENTS

PREFACE

I've always loved auto racing of all kinds, from Formula 1 and stock cars to dragsters and indies. Growing up in Michigan, I don't think there was a year that went by where I didn't watch the Indianapolis 500 or the races at Daytona.

The Detroit Dragway and later the Michigan International Speedway out in Irish Hills became frequent haunts. We saw some amazing races there. Later, I would see races at small dirt tracks throughout the southland—everything from Midgets with Wings to Demolition Derbies.

These men, and now women, push the boundaries of speed and competition in the scorching summer sun across America and especially the South. Visit these small racetracks, and you step back in time.

This is the story of the gutsy drivers and their speed machines during the golden age of stock car racing on everything from dirt tracks to concrete ovals across the Southland of America. In the sweltering summer sun, they fought for money, reputation, glory and of course, 'bragging rights'.

And the only thing that had more wear and tear on it than the cars were the drivers. Some say that a driver would actually lose several pounds during a 500-lap race. And while these might look like the average automobile inside, these were cars on steroids reaching speeds in excess of 200mph.

The roar of engines filled the crisp morning air, a symphony of power and ambition as drivers in their sleek, brightly colored machines prepared for the race ahead. It was the 1960s, a golden era of auto racing where the spirit of competition mingled with the scent of burning rubber and high-octane fuel. Men, their faces set with steely determination and sweat, donned their helmets, ready to dance with death on the asphalt. The track, a serpent of pavement winding through verdant countryside, lay ahead like a gauntlet thrown down by the gods of speed. As the flag dropped, tires screeched, and hearts pounded, the cars surged forward, leaving behind a blur of metal and dreams in their wake.

From the smell of peanuts, beer, and cotton candy to gasoline, burning rubber, and human sweat, it was a special time and place when the new sport of stock car racing came into being. This is their story of competition, camaraderie, and culture.

Goodyear, God, and Gatorade were the watchwords then, and they still are today.

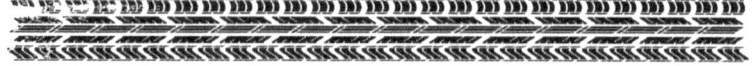

FOREWARD

The crowd buzzed with anticipation, a sea of spectators clad in everything from tailored suits to floral sundresses, their eyes gleaming with excitement and a hint of fear. The grandstands vibrated with the collective heartbeat of thousands, all eager to witness the spectacle of man versus machine. Pit crews bustled with frenetic energy, making final adjustments to engines that purred like caged beasts, ready to unleash their fury.

As the flag dropped, a split-second of silence hung in the air before the explosive symphony of tires screeching and engines roaring erupted. The cars surged forward, a blur of metal and dreams, each driver pushing the limits of speed and skill. They weaved through the first turn, mere inches from disaster, the smell of gasoline and burning rubber intoxicating in its raw intensity.

Every corner of the track held the potential for triumph or catastrophe. The drivers, their hands steady on the wheel and eyes laser-focused, navigated the treacherous curves and straightaways with a mix of calculated precision and fearless abandon. The world beyond the track faded into oblivion, replaced by the singular, all-consuming pursuit of victory. And it was not just competition at the track races were a regular community event.

Spectators held their breath as the leaders jostled for position, engines roaring louder with each desperate push for the front. The sun climbed higher in the sky, casting shadows that danced with the speeding cars. Amidst the mechanical ballet, there was an artistry to the way the drivers maneuvered, each subtle movement a testament to their unparalleled skill and courage.

In the pits, mechanics and crew chiefs watched with bated breath, ready to spring into action at a moment's notice. A quick pit stop could mean the difference between winning and losing, and every second counted. Tires were changed with lightning speed, fuel tanks filled with precision, and drivers sent back into the fray, their cars roaring back to life as they rejoined the race.

The finish line drew nearer with each lap, the tension mounting as the race reached its climax. The air was electric, charged with the raw energy of competition. Fans leaned forward, eyes wide with anticipation, as the leaders rounded the final turn. It was a blur of speed, a culmination of courage, skill, and sheer willpower. The checkered flag waved, and as the victor crossed the line, a triumphant cheer erupted, echoing across the track.

In that moment, the world stood still. The 1960s, with its heady mix of danger and glory, had once again crowned a champion. And as the cars rolled to a stop and the drivers emerged, faces streaked with sweat and grime, the legend of that day would be

etched into the annals of racing history, a testament to the indomitable spirit of those who dared to chase the dream of speed. This is their story of speed, skill and gasoline!

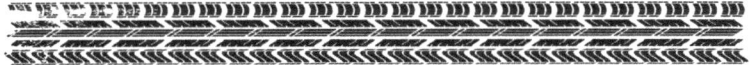

CHAPTER 1

Goodyear, God, and Gatorade
Hot Fun in the Summertime!

"No, no, he didn't slam you, he didn't bump you, he
didn't nudge you... he rubbed you.
And rubbin', son, is racin'!"
Harry Hogge, 'Days of Thunder'

The summer sun was a relentless ball of fire, hanging low in the Carolina sky. The cicadas droned their incessant symphony as if trying to outdo the roar of the engines that would soon fill the air. Thunder Road Raceway, an oval dirt track carved out of a forgotten piece of farmland, stood as a monument to speed and rebellion. It was here, in this red clay crucible, that men tested their mettle and machines bared their steel souls.

Bobby 'Hot shoe' Harris adjusted the brim of his grease-stained cap, shading his eyes from the glare as he surveyed the pit. His '57 Chevy, its blue paint now a patchwork of scrapes and primer, sat in the garage bay like a bull waiting for the gate to open.

To Bobby, that car was more than a machine. It was an extension of his very being, a testament to hours spent under the hood, tweaking, tuning, and coaxing every ounce of horsepower from its roaring V8 engine.

"She ready, Bobby?" came a voice from behind. Bobby turned to see Jimmy 'Rook' Mitchell, one of his best friends and his Chief Mechanic, wiping his hands on an oily rag.

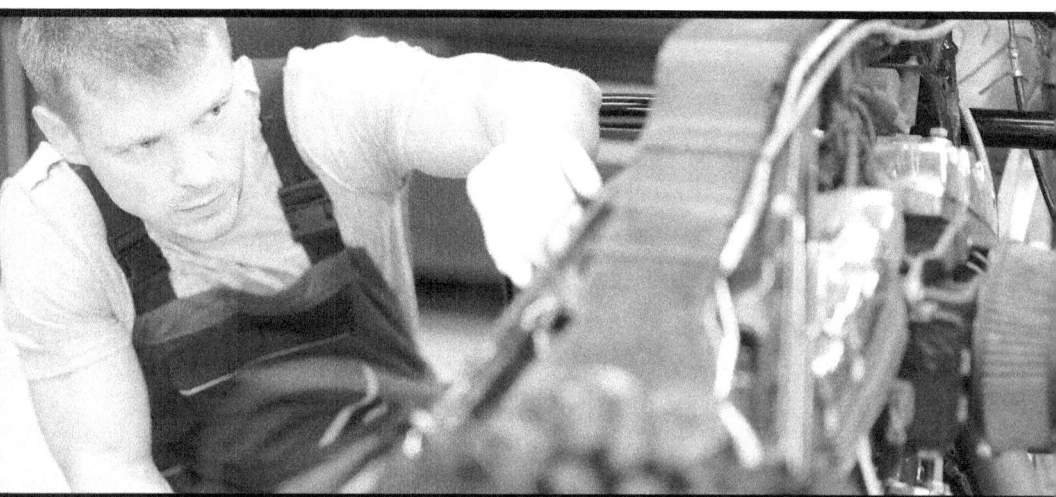

"Ready as she'll ever be," Bobby replied, a grin spreading across his face. "How about you? You got that fuel mixture dialed in just right?"

Jimmy nodded, tossing the rag aside. "Got it purring like a kitten. She'll fly tonight."

The two men stood in companionable silence, listening to the sounds of the track waking up around them. Other drivers were arriving, trailers creaking under the weight of their prized machines, the air thick with the smell of gasoline and rubber.

Bobby's mind wandered back to the first time he felt the thrill of the race. He was just a boy then, perched on the fence with wide eyes as the cars screamed past. His father, a moonshiner with a talent for outrunning the law, had taken him to the races every chance he got. It was there, amidst the dust and chaos, that Bobby fell in love with the pure, unadulterated power of stock car racing.

"Hey, Bobby!" a voice called out, snapping him back to the present. It was Chet Daniels, the track announcer, his voice as gravelly as the track itself. "You ready to give 'em hell tonight?"

Bobby laughed, slapping Chet on the back. "You know it, Chet. Ain't no other way to live!" Chet grinned, his eyes twinkling with the mischief of a man who'd seen it all. "Good luck out there. You're gonna need it with the competition tonight."

Bobby nodded, the weight of the challenge settling on his shoulders. The competition was fierce, with drivers from all over the South converging on Thunder Road for a shot at glory. Men like Red Dawson, a seasoned veteran with a penchant for dirty tricks, and Johnny 'Wildcat' Walker, a hotheaded newcomer with a chip on his shoulder.

As the sun dipped below the horizon, Bobby felt a familiar surge of adrenaline. This was his world, his stage, and tonight he would hold nothing back and leave everything on that track.

The stock car sat low and aggressive, its sleek body glistening under the track lights. Bold sponsor decals covered the exterior, vibrant against the polished metal. The engine, a beast of raw power, rumbled beneath the hood, promising speed and adrenaline. Inside, the cockpit was stripped down, all business—roll cage, harness, and gauges gleaming like instruments of war. This machine was built for one thing: to race, to push limits, to transform drivers into gladiators of the asphalt.

"Time to suit up, Rook," he said, hitting Jimmy on the shoulder. "Let's show 'em what we got."

Jimmy nodded, his face set in determination. Together, they climbed into the Chevy, the engine rumbling to life with a throaty growl. Bobby tightened his grip on the steering wheel, his heart pounding in time with the roar of the engine.

As the cars lined up for the first heat, the crowd's anticipation was palpable. The green flag dropped, and with it, the race began. Bobby's world narrowed to the confines of the track, the roar of the engines, and the pounding of his heart. This was his domain, his battlefield, and he was ready. But there was just one complication. Well, actually there was soon to be three of them but…

The hymn of the NW Florida countryside was a distant murmur outside their farm house window, built in 1907; it was a faint reminder of the world long gone. Mary sat at the kitchen table, her meal untouched as her fingers traced the rim of her coffee mug, the steam curling up in delicate spirals. She was lost in thought, her mind drifting to a future she yearned to grasp—a home filled with the laughter of children, the warmth of suppers at the table, the chaos of bedtime routines... family stuff.

Meanwhile, Bobby stood by the window, his gaze fixed on the horizon where the skyline met the setting sun. His heart raced with the thought of roaring engines and the thrill of a race track. The

smell of burning rubber and the adrenaline-fueled moments of pure speed haunted his dreams, filling him with an almost palpable longing. Racing wasn't just a passion– it was his calling. But here, in the quiet, that dream seemed as far away as the horizon he couldn't really reach.

"Bobby," Mary said softly, her voice a gentle nudge back to reality. He turned to face her, his eyes still glazed with the remnants of his daydream. "We need to talk." This was never a good sign.

He knew what was coming. They'd been skirting around this conversation for months, each lost in their own desires, each afraid of the compromise it would demand. He walked over to the table, pulling out a chair and sitting down, his fingers drumming a nervous rhythm on the wood surface.

"I want a family, Bob," Mary said, her voice trembling slightly. "I want us to have a home, to build something solid together that lasts."

Bobby sighed, running a hand through his unruly hair. "I know, honey, but racing... it's my dream. I've been working so hard to get a spot on the circuit. It's everything I've ever wanted and we are soooo close."

Mary's eyes glistened with unshed tears. "But what about us? What about our dreams? Can't we find a way to make both work?"

He reached across the old wooden table, taking her hand in his. "I don't know how, Mary. Racing is demanding. It's dangerous. It takes everything you've got. I can't be half-hearted about it. And raising a family... that's a full-time commitment too. But I know God would not lead me down this road only to have me turn back now. I honesty believe that," he said.

They sat in silence, the weight of their unspoken fears and unfulfilled dreams hanging heavy in the air. Mary squeezed his hand, trying to bridge the gap between their hearts. "I don't want to lose you, Bobby. But I also don't want to lose myself in a life that feels somehow incomplete."

He looked into her eyes, seeing the depth of her love and the pain of their conflicting desires. "I love you, Mary, more than anything. But I'm scared. Scared that I'll regret not chasing this dream, and scared that I'll fail you if I do."

The countryside outside grew darker, the lights flickering on one by one, mirroring the uncertainty within their hearts. Mary took a deep breath, her resolve hardening. "We have to find a way. Maybe it's not all or nothing. Maybe we can support each other in our dreams and find some middle ground."

Bobby nodded slowly, hope flickering in his eyes. "Maybe we can. But it'll be hard. Really hard."

"Yeah *life* is hard, Bobby, but it's also beautiful. And I believe in us. I believe with God's help we can make it all work, somehow," she said.

Their hands remained intertwined, a symbol of their commitment to each other, even in the face of uncertainty. They knew the road ahead would be rocky, filled with compromises and sacrifices. But in that moment, they chose to believe in their love, in their shared strength, and in the possibility of a future where both their dreams could coexist.

The night deepened, and as they sat together, the distant murmur chickens settling in for the night faded into the background, leaving only the sound of their breaths, in unison, a promise to face whatever came next, together.

Mary thought it best that she wait to tell him that he was going to be a father until a little bit later.

CHAPTER 2

Rivalries and Rumbles
Hot Temps and Hot Tempers

*"Driving a race car is like dancing
with a chainsaw."*
Cale Yarborough

The first heat ended with Bobby taking second place, a respectable start but not enough to quench his thirst for victory. The night air cooled as the crowd settled into the rhythm of the races, the excitement building with each lap. In the pit, Bobby and Jimmy worked tirelessly, fine-tuning the Chevy for the main event.

"She's running a little hot," Jimmy said, wiping sweat from his brow. "Might need to adjust the timing a bit or maybe a bigger gap in the sparks."

Bobby nodded, his focus unyielding. "Do what you gotta do. We can't afford any mistakes."

As Jimmy tinkered with the engine, Bobby scanned the crowd. He spotted his wife, Mary, in the stands, her smile a beacon of support. She waved, and he waved back, drawing strength from her unwavering faith in him. Beside her sat their son, Tommy, his eyes wide with admiration. Bobby felt a pang of self-respect. He was racing not just for himself, but also for his family and his fans.

"Hey, Hotshoe," a voice sneered. Bobby turned to see Red Dawson sauntering over, his swagger as pronounced as the tobacco bulge in his cheek. "Nice run out there. Shame you couldn't keep up."

Bobby clenched his jaw, forcing a smile. "Race ain't over yet, Red. We'll see who crosses that finish line first."

Red laughed, a harsh, grating sound. "Just don't choke, Harris. Wouldn't want to disappoint the little lady."

Bobby's fists tightened, but he forced himself to stay calm. Red was trying to get under his skin, and he wouldn't give him the satisfaction. Instead, he turned back to the car, focusing on his task.

"Ignore him, Bobby," Jimmy said, not really looking up from his work. "He's just scared you're gonna beat him. To hell with him!"

Bobby nodded, letting out a slow breath. "Yeah, you're right. Let's finish this."

The local dirt track hummed with a sense of community as dusk settled over the worn bleachers and makeshift concessions. Families gathered in clusters, the scent of grilled burgers and cotton candy drifting through the air, blending with the earthy aroma of freshly turned dirt. Children dashed around with miniature flags, their faces painted in team colors, eagerly anticipating the roar of engines.

The track itself was a patchwork of worn clay, marked with the scars of countless races—a canvas where local heroes and aspiring champions alike would test their mettle. Old pickup trucks and weathered trailers lined the infield, each bearing the logo of a loyal sponsor or a beloved driver.

As the first cars thundered onto the track, engines reverberating against the backdrop of rolling hills, cheers erupted from the stands. Each lap brought a crescendo of excitement, the crowd leaning forward as cars jostled for position, kicking up plumes of dust that caught the last rays of the setting sun dancing in the light.

In this corner of the world, under the fading light, dreams were born and fates were decided in a swirl of dirt and determination. The announcer's voice crackled over the speakers, narrating the unfolding drama, while flags waved frantically, signaling victory and defeat in equal measure. Here, amidst the simplicity and fervor of local racing, hearts raced as fast as the cars themselves, bound by a shared passion for speed and the thrill of the chase.

The main event loomed, the tension mounting as the final preparations were made. The cars lined up on the starting grid, engines revving, the collective roar a symphony of power and aggression. Bobby tightened his grip on the wheel, his pulse quickening. This was it. The moment he'd been working for, dreaming of, ever since he was a boy on that fence watching the cars go around.

The green flag waved, and they were off. The Chevy surged forward, tires biting into the dirt, the roar of the engine drowning out everything else. Bobby's focus narrowed, the world outside the track fading into insignificance. He jockeyed for position, trading paint with Red and Johnny, every move calculated, every decision split-second.

Lap after lap, the battle raged. Red tried to force Bobby into the wall, but Bobby held his ground, retaliating with a nudge that sent Red fishtailing. Johnny, aggressive and reckless, dove into every corner, his car sliding dangerously close to Bobby's.

As the laps wound down, Bobby found himself in the lead, but Red was right on his tail. The final turn approached, and Bobby knew this was it. He had to nail it, or risk losing everything. He pushed the Chevy to its limits, feeling the tires grip, the engine scream, and then—freedom.

He shot out of the turn, the finish line in sight. Red was still there, but it was too late. Bobby crossed the line, the checkered flag waving, the crowd erupting in cheers. He'd done it. He'd won.

The pit was a frenzy of celebration. Jimmy hugged him; Mary and Tommy rushed over, their faces brimming with swag. Bobby lifted Tommy onto his shoulders, feeling a surge of emotion. This was what it was all about—the thrill of the race, the taste of victory, and the love of his family.

But as he looked out over the track, he knew this was just the beginning. The road ahead was long, filled with more races, more challenges, more rivalries. And Bobby 'Hot Shoe' Harris, was ready for every minute and mile of it.

The 1960s South

In the heat of a Southern summer, when the cicadas sang their endless dirge and the kudzu vines threatened to swallow entire towns, men turned to stock car racing. It was the 1960s, a time of transition and turmoil, and in the South, racing wasn't just a sport; it was a way of life.

It was a region undergoing profound social, political, and cultural transformations, driven largely by the Civil Rights Movement. The decade was marked by significant events and shifts in attitudes and policies that sought to address centuries of racial injustice and segregation.

The 1960s saw crucial milestones such as the sit-ins that began in Greensboro, North Carolina, in 1960,

where black students protested segregated lunch counters.

Martin Luther King Jr., a central figure, led nonviolent protests, including the 1963 Birmingham Campaign and the 1965 Selma to Montgomery marches. The March on Washington in 1963, where King delivered his iconic 'I Have a Dream' speech, highlighted the demand for racial equality and economic justice.

Legislation
The Civil Rights Act of 1964, signed by President Lyndon B. Johnson, outlawed discrimination based on race, color, religion, sex, or national origin,

effectively ending segregation in America.

The Voting Rights Act of 1965 targeted discriminatory practices that had disenfranchised African Americans, particularly in the South, by prohibiting racial discrimination in voting.

Resistance & Violence
The movement faced fierce resistance. White supremacist groups, including the Ku Klux Klan, were active, and violence was rampant. Notable incidents include the bombing of the 16th Street Baptist Church in Birmingham in 1963, which killed four young African American girls, and the murder of civil rights workers in Mississippi during the Freedom Summer of 1964. It was a time of change and it came slowly to most places especially the racetracks of the south.

Social & Economic Change
Education and Integration
Following the Supreme Court's 1954 Brown v. Board of Education decision, efforts to desegregate schools met with both progress and opposition. Notable struggles included the Little Rock Nine in 1957 and the University of Mississippi's violent riots when James Meredith enrolled as its first black student in 1962. Urbanization and Industrialization increased and the South began to see economic changes as it moved away from its traditional agricultural base. Urbanization increased, and new

industries emerged, leading to shifts in the workforce and economic dynamics.

Cultural Shifts:

Music & Literature

The 1960s Southern culture was deeply influenced by music, with genres like blues, jazz, and the emerging sounds of Southern rock and soul gaining popularity. Artists such as Aretha Franklin and Otis Redding played significant roles.

Southern literature continued to reflect the region's complexities, with writers like Harper Lee, whose 1960 novel "To Kill a Mockingbird" explored racial injustice, and William Faulkner, whose works delved into the South's historical burdens.

Changing Attitudes

The civil rights movement gradually shifted public opinion on race relations. While deep-seated prejudices and segregationist attitudes persisted among many, there was a growing acknowledgment of the need for racial equality.

Political Landscape:
Shifts in Political Power
The 1960s saw changes in the political dynamics of the South. The Democratic Party, traditionally dominant in the region, began to fracture over civil rights issues, leading to the rise of the Republican Party, which capitalized on the growing discontent among white conservatives.

Prominent Leaders
Figures like George Wallace, the segregationist governor of Alabama, symbolized the old guard's resistance, while new leaders emerged advocating for civil rights and social change.

The South in the 1960s was a region in the midst of a dramatic and often tumultuous transformation for the first time in a century.. On the racetracks of the region change was slow in coming. NASCAR only banned the Confederate flag in 2020. From Mechanics and driver to owners and officials, Blacks were rare in racing… both then and now.

CHAPTER 3

The Road to Glory?
Hot Fun in the Summertime!

*"If you think the last four words of the national
anthem are 'Gentlemen, start your engines!'
You just might be a Redneck!"*
Comedian Jeff Foxworthy

With the taste of victory fresh in his mouth, Bobby
Harris couldn't help but feel a sense of invincibility.
The win at Thunder Road Raceway had cemented
his reputation as a force to be reckoned with, but the
racing circuit was an unforgiving mistress. Glory
was fleeting, and there was always another race,
another challenger ready to knock you off your
pedestal and take your rep down a notch.

A few weeks later, Bobby found himself at the
Darlington Raceway, a sprawling asphalt track
known for its treacherous turns and fierce
competition. This race was different—bigger, faster,
more prestigious. The Southern 500 drew the best
drivers from across the country, each one hungry for
the title and the winners circle.

As Bobby and Jimmy unloaded the Chevy from the
trailer, the atmosphere was electric. The stands were
already filling with fans, the smell of fried food and
gasoline mingling in the air. Bobby felt the familiar

rush of adrenaline, the anticipation of the race coursing through his veins.

"Think we're ready for this, Rook?" Bobby asked, casting a glance at Jimmy.

Jimmy nodded, a determined look in his eyes. "We've done everything we can. It's really all up to you now. Do or die time!" Bobby grinned, slapping his friend on the back. "Let's go win us a race."

In the garage area, drivers and crews buzzed with activity. Bobby exchanged nods and handshakes with familiar faces, but there was an undercurrent of tension. This was the big leagues, and every driver here was a potential rival.

"Hot Shoe Harris," came a voice. Bobby turned to see a tall man with a confident stride approaching. It was Roy "Rocket" Stevens, a seasoned driver with a string of victories under his belt. "Heard you had a good run at old Thunder Road. Think you can really keep up with the big boys?"

Bobby smiled, his eyes narrowing. "Only one way to find out, Rocket." Roy chuckled, slapping Bobby on the shoulder and wiping his peanut juice on his shirt. "I'll see ya'll out there for sure. Just try not to eat too much of my dust." As Roy walked away, Jimmy leaned in. "He's good. But you're better. Don't let him psych you out." Bobby nodded, his confidence unwavering. "I know. Let's make sure the car's 110% perfect."

The hours leading up to the race were a blur of activity. Jimmy went over every inch of the Chevy, making adjustments, double-checking settings, and ensuring everything was in top condition. Bobby sat in the driver's seat, going through his mental checklist, visualizing track and competition.

When the call to the starting line finally came, Bobby felt a calm settle over him. This was his moment. The grandstands were packed, the crowd a sea of faces, all waiting for the thunderous roar of engines that signaled the start of the race.

He pulled the Chevy into position, the rumble of the engine a steady reassurance. To his left, Rocket Stevens sat in his Ford, his face a mask of concentration. To his right, Johnny Walker revved his engine, a cocky grin on his face. Bobby tightened his grip on the wheel, his heart pounding.

The green flag dropped, and the cars surged forward, a cacophony of sound and motion. Bobby pushed the Chevy hard, the tires gripping the asphalt as he fought for position. The first few laps were a chaotic dance, cars jostling for space, engines roaring with the smell of burning rubber in the air.

Bobby settled into a rhythm, his focus razor-sharp. He maneuvered through the pack, each pass a calculated risk. Rocket Stevens was ahead, his Ford a blur of speed and precision. Bobby knew he had to bide his time, waiting for just the right moment.

The race unfolded in a series of heart-stopping moments. Bobby traded paint with Johnny Walker, their cars brushing against each other as they fought for position. He narrowly avoided a spinout when Red Dawson tried to cut him off, his reflexes sharp, instincts honed.

With ten laps to go, Bobby found himself in third place, Rocket and Johnny ahead of him. The crowd was on its feet, the tension palpable. Bobby pushed the Chevy harder, feeling the engine respond, the car becoming an extension of himself.

He made his move on Johnny first, diving low on a turn, the Chevy's tires squealing in protest. Johnny tried to block, but Bobby was too fast, too determined. He pulled ahead, his eyes now locked on Rocket Stevens.

The final laps were a blur of speed and adrenaline. Rocket and Bobby battled fiercely, their cars inches apart, the lead changing hands with every turn. Bobby could see the determination in Rocket's eyes, but he knew he had something more—an unyielding will to win, a drive born from years of hard work and sacrifice.

On the final lap, Bobby made his move. He timed it perfectly, diving low on the last turn, the Chevy's tires gripping the asphalt with a tenacity that matched his own. Rocket tried to cut him off, but Bobby held his line, the finish line looming ahead.

With a final surge of speed, Bobby crossed the finish line, the checkered flag waving, the crowd erupting in cheers. He had done it. He had won the famous Southern 500.

The pit was a whirlwind of celebration. Jimmy hugged him, tears of joy in his eyes. Mary and Tommy rushed over, their faces beaming with pride. Bobby lifted Tommy onto his shoulders, feeling a surge of emotion.

"You did it, Daddy!" Tommy shouted, his voice filled with awe.

Bobby smiled, tears in his eyes. "We did it, son. *We* did it!"

As he looked out over the track, the magnitude of his achievement sank in. This was more than a victory. It was a testament to his hard work, his determination, and the unwavering support of his family and friends. He had faced the best, and he had come out on top.

Bobby had come a long way from racing the Red Clay Roads. The sun had barely begun its descent when the engines roared to life at Escambia County Raceway in NW Florida. Dust from the red clay track hung in the air, mingling with the scent of burnt rubber and fried food from the concession stands. It was a Saturday ritual, one that folks in this small Southern town held onto with a fierce grip, a defiant stand against the slow march of time and the encroaching modern world outside.

Amid the crowd, teenagers flirted and shared earbuds, listening to rock music that clashed with the roar of the engines. Old men, faces weathered by sun and time, leaned against the rusted fence, swapping stories and betting on drivers who were the grandsons of the men they used to cheer for.

By now Bobby had become the local favorite. He was wiping the grime off his number 77 car, a battered but beloved machine that had seen more wins than the town had seen new faces in the past decade. He was a tall man with a lean build, his eyes as sharp as the curves he conquered each week. His hands moved with practiced ease, the grease and dirt almost part of his skin by now.

"Got her running smooth?" called out Jimmy, his best friend and makeshift mechanic, from under the hood of the car.

"Smooth as she's gonna get," Bobby replied, a crooked grin spreading across his face. He tapped the hood of his car affectionately. "She's ready for another dance with the lady called 'Speed'!."

As the announcer's voice crackled over the PA system, the crowd's murmur grew to a roar. Families settled into their seats, kids holding cotton candy and homemade signs, eyes wide with excitement.

The national anthem played, hats came off, hands over hearts, a moment of calm before the chaos.

The green flag dropped, and the cars shot forward, a blur of colors and noise. Bobby felt that familiar rush, the adrenaline pumping through his veins. It was more than just a race; it was a battle, a dance, a testament to a way of life that refused to fade.

Lap after lap, the dust thickened, and the track seemed to shrink as drivers fought for position. He could feel the tension, the unspoken rivalry, and the camaraderie that only those who danced on the edge of this danger could really fully understand.

As the final lap approached, Bobby saw his chance. He took the inside curve, his car sliding dangerously close to the wall. The crowd held its breath, the world narrowing to this moment, this race, this track. When he crossed the finish line, the cheer was deafening, a collective release of both tension and joy. The party at victory lane was legendary.

Later, in the cool of the evening, after the last car had left the track and the dust had settled, Bobby sat on the hood of his car, looking out over the empty stands. The lights flickered off one by one, and the night swallowed the track in silence. It was a fleeting moment, a brief pause before the cycle began again. But for now, it was enough.

The roar of the engines, the smell of the dirt, the cheers of the crowd—they were the heartbeat of this county, and as long as those things remained, so too did the spirit of this small Southern town.

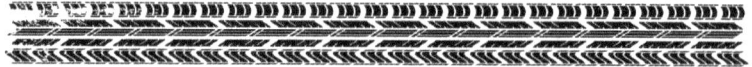

CHAPTER 4

Trials and Tribulations
It's Nice to be First

"If you're in control…
you're not going fast enough."
Parnelli Jones

The glory of Bobby's victory at Darlington was still fresh in the minds of many, but the racing world moved on quickly. Each race brought new challenges, and Bobby knew he couldn't rest on his laurels. The next big race loomed on the horizon, and with it, the pressure to prove this was no fluke.

Back in the small garage that served as their headquarters, Bobby and Jimmy were hard at work. The '57 Chevy had taken a beating at Darlington, and it needed more than a little TLC to be ready for the next race. Bobby wiped the sweat from his brow as he leaned over the engine, his hands greasy and his mind focused.

"Pass me the wrench, Jimmy," Bobby said, his voice muffled as he tightened a bolt. Jimmy handed him the tool, his own hands just as dirty.

"You know, Bobby, this next race is gonna be tough. Talladega's a different beast altogether."

Bobby nodded, his eyes never leaving the engine. "I know. But we've faced tough before. We'll get through it."

Jimmy sighed, leaning against the workbench. "I just want you to be careful. Those speeds, those banks… you know it's dangerous."

Bobby paused, looking up at his friend. "I appreciate it, Jimmy. But you know I can't back down. Not now. Not ever."

The weeks leading up to the race were a blur of preparations and long nights in the garage. Mary brought them meals, her presence a comforting reminder of what Bobby was fighting for. Tommy often sat nearby, watching his father with wide eyes, dreaming of the day he might follow in his footsteps and establish a racing legacy of his own.

But in the meantime Bobby was interested in 'making time' with Mary! The night air was warm, stars shimmering above as they leaned against the hood of the car. He pulled her closer, their bodies illuminated by the soft glow of the streetlights. She felt the cool metal beneath her, a stark contrast to the heat of his touch.

Their lips met, a spark igniting between them. Fingers tangled in hair, breaths mingling, the kiss deepening as they lost themselves in the moment. The world faded away, leaving only the rhythmic thrum of their hearts and the quiet hum of the engine beneath them. This was freedom, passion, and a moment suspended in time, the night wrapping them in its embrace.

Finally, race day arrived. Alabama's Talladega Superspeedway is a behemoth of a track, its steep banks and long straightaways demanding respect from even the most seasoned drivers. The stands are always packed and the atmosphere electric.

As Bobby stood by his car, looking out over the track, he felt a mixture of excitement and trepidation. This race would be a true test of his driving skill and stamina as well as his nerve.
"Bobby," Mary said, coming up beside him. She took his hand, her eyes filled with concern. "Just promise me you'll be careful." He squeezed her

hand, giving her a reassuring smile. "I promise, Mary. I'll do my best." She nodded, though the worry never left her eyes. "I know you will. Just remember, we're here for you. No matter what."

With a final kiss from Mary, Bobby climbed into the Chevy, the roar of the engine drowning out his thoughts. He pulled into position on the starting grid, surrounded by the best drivers in the country. Rocket Stevens, Johnny Walker, Red Dawson—they were all here, each one eager to claim victory.

The green flag dropped, and the cars surged forward, engines screaming. Talladega's high banks and fast straights made for a thrilling, yet perilous, race. Bobby felt the familiar rush of adrenaline as he jockeyed for position. As usual his focus was unwavering as he fought to the front.

In the pits, tension boiled over as two crew members squared off, shouts slicing through the air. Grease-stained hands clenched into fists, eyes locked in a fiery glare. Around them, the hum of engines and chatter of radios faded into the background, all focus on the impending clash.

One lunged first, fists connecting with a sharp crack, sending the other stumbling back into a stack of tires. Shouts erupted from nearby teams, some rushing in to break it up, others egging them on. Tools clattered to the ground, forgotten in the chaos.

The pit, usually a place of precise teamwork, became a battleground. Tempers flared, adrenaline pumping as they grappled, fueled by the heat of the moment. It was a raw, primal scene, a burst of emotion in a world where everything else was controlled, measured, and timed to perfection. Then, as quickly as it ignited, it was over, crews pulling them apart, the track's roar reclaiming the air as focus shifted back to the race.

The laps ticked by in a blur of speed and precision. Bobby found himself in a fierce battle with Rocket and Johnny, the three cars trading places in a high-stakes dance. Each move was calculated, each decision critical. Midway through the race, disaster struck. In a split second, a tire blew on Red Dawson's car, sending him spinning out of control. The track erupted into chaos as cars swerved to avoid the wreck. Bobby narrowly avoided the pileup, his heart pounding as he regained control.

The caution flag came out, and the cars slowed, the tension palpable. Bobby's hands shook slightly as he took a deep breath, trying to calm his nerves. This was the reality of racing—danger lurking around every corner.

As the race resumed, Bobby pushed the Chevy harder, determined to make up for lost ground. The final laps were a blur of speed and adrenaline, the finish line drawing ever closer. In a daring move, Bobby slipped past Rocket on the inside, his tires skimming the edge of control.

With one lap to go, it was a two-man race. Bobby and Johnny, neck and neck, each fighting for every inch. The crowd was on its feet, the roar deafening. Bobby could feel the strain on his car, the engine screaming in protest.

In the final turn, Johnny made his move, diving low in a desperate bid for the lead. Bobby reacted instinctively, holding his line, his focus razor sharp. The finish line loomed ahead, the checkered flag waving him into the money. With a final surge of speed, Bobby "Hot shoe" Harris crossed the finish line first, the crowd erupting in cheers. He had done it. He had won at Talladega!

The victory was sweet, but it came with a sobering reminder of all the risks involved. As Bobby climbed out of the car, the weight of what had happened to Red hit him. The celebration was muted by the reality of the sport's real dangers.

In the aftermath, Bobby found himself reflecting on what truly mattered. The thrill of victory was intoxicating, but it was the love and support of his family and friends that grounded him. As he looked out over the track, Mary and Tommy by his side,

Bobby knew that no matter what challenges lay ahead, he'd face them with the same determination and heart that had served him well.

"Jimmy," Bobby said, leaning against the car. "I've been thinking a lot lately. About the future. About my family."

Jimmy looked up, his brow furrowed. "What

you gettin' at, Bobby? What's the point?"

Bobby took a deep breath. "I love racing, but I love my family more. I can't keep putting them through this. After Charlotte, I'm gonna take a break, spend more time at home. Maybe find ways to stay in the sport *without* driving every week."

Jimmy nodded slowly, understanding dawning in his eyes. "I get it, Bobby. We've been at this a long time. You've got nothing left to prove. Whatever you decide, I'm with you."

The race at Charlotte was a true test of endurance and skill. The miles ticked by slowly, each lap a reminder of the grueling nature of the sport. Bobby pushed the Chevy hard, his focus unwavering, but his mind kept drifting to Mary and Tommy, to the life he wanted to build with them.

During a stock car pit stop, the air vibrates with urgency. Tires screech as the car halts, and the pit crew springs into action like a well-oiled machine. Four tire changers, wielding air guns, converge on the vehicle, removing and replacing tires with precision and speed.

Fuelers swiftly connect hoses, pumping gallons of gasoline in seconds, while the 'Jackman' elevates the car effortlessly, allowing the team to work underneath. A seamless choreography—as wrenches spin and bolts fly.

Above the din, the crew chief watches, eyes darting between the stopwatch and the track, calculating the precious seconds saved or lost. Then, in a heartbeat, it was over—the car roars back onto the track, the crew already preparing for the next pit stop.

The infield pulsed with life, a vibrant tapestry of tents, trailers, and RVs sprawled under the bright sun. Fans milled about, clutching beers and hot dogs, their laughter and chatter mingling with the distant roar of engines. Grills sizzled, sending up tantalizing plumes of smoke that mixed with the scent of freshly cut grass.

Children darted between the legs of adults, waving checkered flags, their faces painted in team colors. Radios blared race commentary, each campsite its own mini-kingdom, adorned with flags and banners of favorite drivers.

Groups gathered around portable TVs, eyes glued to the screen, sharing predictions and banter. A sense of camaraderie hung in the air, a community forged in the shared thrill of speed and competition. As cars zoomed by on the track, a cheer erupted, binding everyone in that moment—a pulse of adrenaline in the heart of the infield.

The crowd's roar faded to a collective gasp as the car spun out of control, tires screeching against asphalt. Metal crumpled, the vehicle slamming into the wall with a deafening crash. Smoke billowed, a gray plume rising against the blue sky, and debris scattered across the track like shrapnel.

Time seemed to slow, the world narrowing to the chaotic scene unfolding. Safety crews sprinted into action, their fluorescent vests a blur against the smoky haze. Fans leaned forward, breath held, eyes glued to the wreckage as the announcer's voice crackled over the speakers, urgent and tense.

Inside the cockpit, the driver took a breath, hands trembling as adrenaline coursed through his veins. Moments later, he emerged from the wreckage, raising a hand to signal he was okay. Relief washed over the crowd, applause and cheers breaking the tense silence—a reminder of the thin line between triumph and disaster in the high-speed world of racing.

With each lap, Bobby found himself reflecting on the journey that had brought him here. The races, the victories, the rivalries—they were all part of who he was. But so was the love and support of his family, the strength he drew from them.

As the race neared its end, Bobby was in the lead, his driving smooth and controlled. The finish line was in sight, the checkered flag waving. With a final burst of speed, he crossed the line first, the crowd erupting in cheers.

The victory was sweet, but it was also bittersweet. As Bobby climbed out of the car, he knew this was the end of one chapter and the beginning of another. The celebrations were joyous, but Bobby's mind was already on the future.

Back home, Bobby and Mary sat on the porch again, the night air cool and crisp. Tommy was asleep inside, his dreams filled with visions of fast cars and daring races.

"I did it, Mary," Bobby said quietly, his voice filled with emotion. "I won at Charlotte. But more importantly, I've made up my mind. I'm going to take a break from racing, focus on you and Tommy. We'll figure out what comes next… together."

Mary smiled, her eyes shining with love, "I'm so proud of you, Bobby. For everything. We'll get through this together. No matter what."

Bobby felt a weight lift from his shoulders, the future suddenly seeming a little brighter. He had faced the toughest challenges on the track, but now he was ready to face the next chapter of his life with the same determination and heart.

America's 2nd Favorite Pastime!

The National Association for Stock Car Auto Racing, more commonly known as NASCAR, has become one of the most popular forms of motorsports in the United States and around the world. Its origins are rooted in the culture of the American South, where moonshiners and bootleggers would modify their cars to evade the law. Over the decades, NASCAR has grown from these humble beginnings into a multi-billion-dollar industry, captivating millions of fans with high-speed thrills and dramatic races.

Origins & Early Years
NASCAR was officially founded by Bill France Sr. on February 21, 1948. France, a mechanic and auto-repair shop owner, recognized the need for a governing body to regulate stock car racing, which

was becoming increasingly popular in the southeastern United States. Before NASCAR's formation, races were often unorganized and marred by inconsistent rules and unscrupulous promoters.

The first official NASCAR race was held on February 15, 1948, on Daytona Beach, Florida. Red Byron won this race, and he went on to become the first NASCAR champion. The inaugural season featured a series of races on dirt tracks and temporary circuits, emphasizing the accessibility and relatability of stock car racing compared to other motorsports like Formula 1 or IndyCar.

The 1950s: Establishing a Foundation
The 1950s were a formative decade for NASCAR. The first official NASCAR Grand National Series (now the NASCAR Cup Series) race was held on June 19, 1949, at the Charlotte Speedway. Jim Roper won the race driving a Lincoln, symbolizing the early connection between NASCAR and American car manufacturers.

As the decade progressed, NASCAR began to attract more attention and larger crowds. The construction of purpose-built tracks, such as the Darlington Raceway in South Carolina, which opened in 1950, helped standardize the sport and enhance its appeal. These tracks allowed for safer, more exciting races and contributed to the sport's growing legitimacy.

The 1960s: Expansion & Innovation

The 1960s saw NASCAR continue to expand and innovate. One of the most significant developments was the construction of the Daytona International Speedway, which opened in 1959. The 2.5-mile tri-oval track quickly became the sport's flagship venue, hosting the prestigious Daytona 500. The inaugural Daytona 500 in 1959 was won by Lee Petty, further cementing the Petty family's legacy in the sport.

This decade also witnessed the rise of legendary drivers such as Richard Petty, who would go on to become known as "The King" of NASCAR. Petty won his first Daytona 500 in 1964 and claimed multiple championships throughout the decade, contributing to the sport's increasing popularity.

NASCAR also began to embrace technological advancements during this period. The introduction of aerodynamic modifications and the use of purpose-built race cars, rather than strictly stock models, allowed for faster and more competitive racing. These changes, while controversial to purists, were essential for the sport's growth and the safety of its participants.

The 1970s: Gone Mainstream
The 70s were marked by NASCAR's rise to mainstream popularity. Television played a crucial role in this transformation. The first live flag-to-flag broadcast of the Daytona 500 in 1979 brought the sport to a national audience. The race, famously known for a last-lap crash and ensuing fistfight between drivers Cale Yarborough and the Allison brothers, captivated viewers and showcasing the excitement of NASCAR.

Richard Petty continued to dominate this era, winning seven championships and solidifying his status as a NASCAR legend. However, he was not the only star. Drivers like David Pearson, Bobby Allison, and Darrell Waltrip also made significant impacts, creating fierce rivalries and unforgettable moments.

The 1970s also saw NASCAR diversify its schedule, adding more tracks outside the southeastern United States. This expansion helped grow the sport's fan base and made it a national phenomenon.

The 80s: Corporate Growth
The 1980s brought increased corporate sponsorship and commercialization to NASCAR. Companies recognized the marketing potential of associating

with the sport, leading to lucrative sponsorship deals and greater financial stability for teams. This influx of corporate money allowed for advancements in technology and improvements in safety standards.

One of the most iconic sponsorships was the partnership between Richard Petty and STP. This era also saw the rise of Dale Earnhardt, who would become one of NASCAR's most beloved and successful drivers. Known as "The Intimidator," Earnhardt's aggressive driving style and charismatic personality made him a fan favorite. He won his first championship in 1980 and continued to be a dominant force throughout the decade.

The 1980s also marked the introduction of the Winston Cup sponsorship, which brought significant financial backing and stability to the sport. This period laid the groundwork for NASCAR's transition from just a regional pastime to a major national sport.

The 1990s:
Popularity & Tragedy
The 1990s were a period of peak popularity for NASCAR. The sport continued to attract larger audiences, and its fan base became more diverse. The introduction of new tracks in major markets, such as Texas Motor Speedway and Las Vegas Motor Speedway, further expanded NASCAR's reach.

Jeff Gordon emerged as a new superstar in the 1990s. With his boyish good looks and extraordinary talent, Gordon attracted a new generation of fans. He won his first championship in 1995 and went on to win three more before the decade's end.

However, the 1990s were not without tragedy. The death of Dale Earnhardt in a crash on the final lap of the 2001 Daytona 500 was a devastating blow to the sport. Earnhardt's death underscored the dangers of racing and led to significant changes in safety protocols, including the introduction of the HANS device (Head and Neck Support) and improvements to car design and track safety features.

The 2000s: Technological Challenges
The early 2000s saw NASCAR continue to innovate and grow, but also face new challenges. The implementation of the Car of Tomorrow (COT) was a major technological advancement aimed at improving driver safety. Introduced in 2007, the COT featured a reinforced roll cage, energy-absorbing foam, and a more centralized driver position. While the COT enhanced safety, it also

faced criticism for its aesthetics and handling characteristics.

Jimmie Johnson dominated this era, winning an unprecedented five consecutive championships from 2006 to 2010. His success, combined with the continued popularity of drivers like Jeff Gordon and Tony Stewart, kept NASCAR in the national light

However, the 2000s also saw a decline in TV ratings and attendance. The economic recession of 2008 affected sponsorships and team finances, leading to a more challenging environment for smaller teams. NASCAR responded by implementing cost-cutting measures and exploring new ways to engage fans, including the introduction of the Chase for the Sprint Cup, a playoff system.

The 2010s: Diversity Engagement
The 2010s brought efforts to diversify NASCAR's fan base and improve digital engagement. The Drive for Diversity program aimed to attract more minority and female drivers to the sport, with notable graduates like Bubba Wallace and Daniel Suárez making their mark in the Cup Series.

NASCAR also introduced the Gen-6 car in 2013, designed to more closely resemble production cars and improve the racing product. While the new car was well-received, the sport continued to face challenges with declining viewership.

The 2020s: Adapting to Change

The 2020s have seen NASCAR adapt to a rapidly changing world. The COVID-19 pandemic forced the sport to innovate, leading to the introduction of virtual racing through the eNASCAR iRacing Pro Invitational Series. This move kept fans engaged during the pandemic's early months and showcased the potential of esports in motorsports.

NASCAR also made significant changes to its schedule, adding new tracks and formats to create more exciting and diverse racing experiences. With the introduction of the 'Next Gen' car in 2022 the organization improved competition and safety.

Efforts to address social issues also became more prominent, with NASCAR taking a stand against racial injustice and promoting inclusivity. The decision to ban the Confederate flag in 2020 marked a step toward making the sport more welcoming.

A V8 Future

From its roots in the moonshine-running culture of the American South to its status as a global motorsport phenomenon, NASCAR has undergone a remarkable evolution. With a rich history of legendary drivers, iconic races, and passionate fans, NASCAR continues as a beloved part of American culture.

Southern Tracks of the 1960's

There are two major types of racetracks; Oval track racing is a form of motorsport that's contested on an oval-shaped race track. An oval track differs from a road course in that the layout resembles an oval with turns in only one direction, and the direction of traffic is almost universally counter-clockwise. Oval tracks are dedicated motorsport circuits, used predominantly in the United States. They often have banked turns and some are not precisely oval, and the tracks can vary in shape.

Major forms of oval track racing include stock car racing, open-wheel racing, sprint car racing, modified car racing, midget car racing and dirt track motorcycles. According to the National Speedway Directory, there are over 700 dirt oval tracks in operation in the US. The composition of the dirt on tracks has an effect on the amount of grip available. Many tracks use clay with a mixture of dirt others use the more modern Asphalt surface.
Some of the more popular race tracks of the south during the 1960s and 1970s were;

Air Base Speedway, Greenville, SC

Asheville-Weaverville Speedway, NC
Atlanta Motor Speedway, GA
Augusta Speedway, GA
Cowtown Speedway, TX
Birmingham Fairgrounds Raceway, AL
Bristol Motor Speedway, TN
Central City Speedway, GA
Darlington Raceway, SC
Dixie Speedway, AL
Riverside Speedway, GA
Meyer Speedway, TX
Palm Beach Speedway, FL
Princess Anne Race Course, VA
Lakewood Speedway, GA
Hollis Speedway, AL
North Wilkesboro Speedway, NC
Southern Raceway, FL

Pelican Int'l Speedway, LA
Mountain View Speedway, TN
Hattisburg Race Course, MS
Cherokee Speedway, SC
5 Flags Raceway, FL
North Wilkesboro, NC
Martinsville Speedway, VA
Corpus Christi Speedway, TX

A RACING VOCABULARY

NASCAR has a lingo all its own. Here's a guide to understanding what's being said:

•*Aero-push:* The reduction of front-wheel traction for trailing cars in packs of traffic.

•*Aero-drag:* Devices that don't deflect wind and cause a car to slow down.

•*Bear Grease:* Materials use to patch cracks and small holes in the track that tend to get slippery when it's hot.

•*Back Marker:* Slowpokes that ride at the back of traffic and get in the way of faster cars.

•*Bump-draft:* Two cars lined up a nose-to-tail tandem with the second car pushing the first.

•*Camber:* When a wheel is tilted inward or outward from vertical.

•*Chassis:* The basic skeleton of a car, including the interior, roll cage, bottom of car.

•*Chattering:* When the tires are on the verge of losing grip.

•*Dirty Air:* Turbulence behind lead cars in a pack of traffic.

•*Donuts:* Rubber circles on the side of a car created by a tire when two cars rub.

•*Downforce:* Created aerodynamically and mechanically to create traction.

•*Draft:* The slipstream created when cars line up nose-to-tail. Cars in the draft are much faster than a single car because the group of cars can divide the wind resistance.

•*Greenhouse*: The driver compartment.

•*Groove*: Preferred and fastest racing line.

•*Handling:* The amount of traction gained or lost in the turns.

•*Happy Hour:* Final practice session.

•*Loading:* The amount of downforce applied to any of the tires when it enters or exits a corner

•*Loose:* When the rear tires lose grip.

•*Lucky Dog:* The first car a lap down that's allowed to get back on the lead lap during a caution. The rule was put into place to keep drivers from racing during a yellow flag.

•*Marbles:* Small balls of used tire rubber and debris near the outside and inside walls

•Setup: How the car's suspension is adjusted before and during the race.

•*Scuffs:* Used tires that have been put through one heat cycle to make them harder.

•*Side Draft:* Running side-by-side to gain momentum in another car's wake, much like being behind a boat.

•*Splash-and-Go:* A quick stop for just enough gasoline to finish the race.

•*Splitter:* A metal strip along the bottom of the front of the car to provide downforce.

•*Stickers:* New tires with Goodyear Tire and Rubber Co. stickers on them.

•Stop-and-Go: A NASCAR penalty that requires a driver to stop on pit road before returning to the race track.

•*Sway Bar:* Also known as an anti-roll bar that restricts how much a car "leans" to the right.

•*Tight:* Also known as "push." When the front tires lose grip to affect steering.

•*Track bar:* A rear suspension bar that runs side-to-side that tilts the car left or right.

•*Trading paint:* Aggressive driving when cars bounce into each other. Also known as 'rubbing and bumping.'

•*Valiance:* Plastic front bumper cover that extends to the ground.

•*Wedge:* The adjustable height of the rear springs that affects the attitude of the car.

CHAPTER 5

Cross Roads
Racin in the Southland

"Folks began racing automobiles, the day they built the second automobile!"
Richard Petty

The dirt and asphalt oval racetracks of the South spread out like a network of veins through the rural heartland, each one a vital, dusty artery pulsing with life every Friday and Saturday night. At the edge of sleepy towns, nestled between fields of cotton and corn, these tracks were raw and untamed, carved

from the earth itself. Under the glow of floodlights, the dirt kicks up in clouds, hanging in the air like memories of a simpler time. The sound of roaring engines is a constant hum, a background noise to the conversations and cheers of the crowds in the stands.

The track is filled with a patchwork of humanity: old men in overalls sipping beer, young couples on first dates, and families with wide-eyed children experiencing the thrill of racing for the first time. The scent of fried food mingles with the sweet, metallic tang of gasoline, creating an olfactory tapestry that is unmistakably Southern.

Drivers, modern-day gladiators in their colorful suits, pace around their machines with a mix of reverence and determination. The cars, stripped down to their essentials, are beasts of burden ready to be unleashed. Each race is a test of skill and grit, a dance on the edge of control as drivers navigate the unpredictable terrain, their cars fishtailing, spitting out plumes of dirt and gravel.

Victory here is earned in sweat and dust, and the celebrations are raucous and heartfelt. Winners are embraced like prodigal sons, their triumphs becoming part of the track's lore, retold in the hushed tones of those who witnessed it firsthand. The dirt racetrack is more than just a venue; it's a crucible where the spirit of the South is forged and re-forged, week after week, race after race. His victories at Darlington and Talladega had solidified Bobby's status as one of the top drivers in the circuit, but the toll of racing was beginning to weigh on him. The high-speed chases, the crashes, the ever-present danger—it was a constant test of his endurance and resolve. The late nights in the garage, the long hours, the road, and the endless cycle of races left little time for anything.

One evening, as the sun set over their modest home, Bobby sat on the porch with Mary. The crickets chirped in the distance, and the scent of honeysuckle filled the air. Tommy was playing with his toy cars in the yard, his laughter a sweet melody for all to hear. They were at peace for the for the first time in a very long time.

"Bobby, I've been thinking," Mary said softly, breaking the comfortable silence. She took his hand, her eyes searching his. "You've talked about curtailing your racing but you've continued pushing yourself so hard. Maybe it's time to really slow down a bit, spend more time with us?"

Bobby sighed, his gaze drifting to the horizon. "I know, Mary. I've been thinking about backing off too. But racing is in my blood, its an addiction pure and simple but… I don't want to miss out on Tommy growing up and I have already missed a lot. And I don't want to put you through the worry every time I get behind the wheel. It's just not worth it anymore. At the same time there are dozens of folks who depend on me now to earn a living and I can't let them down. The more I win..."

Mary squeezed his hand, her expression tender. "I love you, Bobby. And you know we'll support you no matter what. But we *do* need you here with us, safe, sane and in one piece!"

Bobby nodded, a mix of emotions swirling inside him. The allure of racing was undeniable, but so was the love he felt for his family. He knew he had to find a balance, a way to pursue his passion without sacrificing the ones he loved.

The next race was again back at the famous Charlotte Motor Speedway, a track known for its grueling 600-mile race. As Bobby and Jimmy prepared the Chevy, the usual excitement was tinged with a sense of contemplation. This race would be a turning point, one way or another.

"Jimmy," Bobby said, leaning against the car. "I've been thinking a lot lately. About the future. About my family." Jimmy looked up, his brow furrowed.

"What are you getting at, Bobby?"

Bobby took a deep breath. "I love racing, but I love my family more. I can't keep putting them through this. After Charlotte, I'm gonna take a break, spend more time at home. Maybe find a way to stay in the sport without driving every week."

Jimmy nodded slowly, understanding dawning in his eyes. "I get it, Bobby. We've been at this a long time. You've got nothing left to prove. Whatever you decide, I'm with you."

Racing at Charlotte was always a test of endurance and skill. The miles ticked by slowly, each lap a reminder of the grueling nature of the sport. Bobby pushed the Chevy hard, his focus unwavering, but his mind kept drifting to Mary and Tommy, to the life he wanted to build with them.

The pits buzzed with a frenetic energy, a symphony of clanking tools and shouted commands. Mechanics in oil-stained coveralls darted between cars, their hands blurs as they changed tires and tightened bolts. The air was thick with the smell of racing and old fashion fun.

Crew chiefs, eyes hidden behind mirrored sunglasses, scanned screens and radios, deciphering data that could make or break their driver's race. Each team worked in unison, a choreography of precision and speed, the seconds ticking down in their minds like a countdown.

Engines roared to life, sending vibrations through the ground. Drivers sat in their cockpits, helmets on, visors down, eyes focused ahead. In this controlled chaos, a sense of anticipation crackled like static electricity. The pits weren't just a stop; they were a battleground where races could be won or lost, a dance of skill and strategy unfolding in front of him.

With each lap, Bobby found himself again reflecting on the journey that had brought him to this point. The races, the victories, the rivalries—they were all part of who he was now. But so was the love and support of his family and the strength from them.

As the race neared its end, Bobby was in the lead, his driving smooth and controlled. The finish line was in sight, the checkered flag waving. With a final burst of speed, he crossed the line first, the crowd erupting in cheers.

Victory lane shimmered under the flood lights, a sanctuary of celebration amidst the echoing roar of engines and the pulsing energy of the crowd. The winning car, adorned with confetti and sponsor decals, stood proudly at the center, a symbol of triumph and perseverance. Champagne corks popped, spraying fizzy arcs of celebration as mechanics and crew members gathered around, their faces lit with euphoria.

Bobby emerged, helmet off, eyes gleaming with disbelief and elation. Cheers erupted from the grandstands, fans waving flags and banners in a symphony of jubilation. Cameras flashed, capturing the moment for eternity as the driver climbed atop the car, arms raised in victory. In victory lane, time seemed suspended, every emotion heightened—the culmination of months of preparation, strategy, and heart-stopping moments on the track. Trophies gleamed in the spotlight, glinting with the promise of glory. For the driver, it was a moment of validation, a reward for pushing boundaries, daring greatly, and emerging victorious in the relentless pursuit of excellence on the asphalt. And winning was just plain fun!

The victory was sweet as they always are, but this one was also a little bittersweet. As Bobby climbed out of the car, he knew this was the end of one chapter and the beginning of another. The celebrations were joyous, but Bobby's mind was made up and already on the future.

Back home, Bobby and Mary sat on the porch again, the night air cool and crisp. Tommy was asleep inside, his dreams filled with boyish visions of fast cars and daring races.

"I did it, Mary," Bobby said quietly, his voice filled with emotion. "I won and we did everything we set on doin. But more importantly, I've made up my mind. I'm finally going to follow thru and take a break from racing... focus on you and Tommy for awhile. We'll figure out what comes next and we'll do it together," he said with a smile.

Bobby felt a weight lift from his shoulders, the future suddenly seeming a little brighter. He had faced the toughest challenges on the track, but now he was ready to face the next chapter of his life with the same determination and heart.

Mary smiled, her eyes shining with love and pride. "I'm so proud of you, Bobby. For everything. We'll get through this together. No matter what."

As she drifted off to sleep that evening Mary reminisced about growing up here in this sleepy NW Florida town…

The heat of the southern sun pressed down like a heavy hand on the small dirt racetrack. Each summer day seemed to stretch endlessly, the cicadas' chorus rising in the thick air. The sweet scent of honeysuckle and magnolia blooms lingered, mingling with the earthy aroma of freshly plowed fields. These were places where time ambled, and the past was never far away.

In a creaking, white-painted house on the edge of town, young Mary grew up with a curious spirit and wide, inquisitive eyes. Her days were a picture of simple pleasures and small-town dramas. Mornings began with the rooster's crow, the sound echoing across the open fields, mingling with the distant murmur of the Tennessee River.

Mary's world was defined by the red clay roads and the cotton fields that stretched to the horizon. She would race her brothers down the dusty paths, their laughter ringing out as they chased each other past the old pecan trees that lined their route. The air was always warm, the sky a vast expanse of blue, occasionally punctuated by drifting clouds.

The School was a single-story brick building that smelled of chalk and books. The classrooms were filled with rows of wooden desks, each carved with the initials of generations of students. Mrs. Thompson, the teacher, was a stern woman with a kind heart hidden beneath her strict exterior. She taught them about a world far beyond the borders of their little town, though it was hard to imagine anything more captivating than their own world.

Sunday mornings were sacred, a ritual that began with the ringing of the church bell, calling the faithful to the white-steepled building at the town's center. The congregation was a sea of starched shirts and floral dresses, the women fanning themselves against the oppressive heat as the preacher's voice rose and fell, weaving tales of redemption and hope. Yet, beneath the placid surface of Mary's childhood, the 1960s were stirring with change.

The adults spoke in hushed tones about the Civil Rights Movement, their voices tinged with fear and hope. Like many southern towns, this was a place of deep traditions, and the winds of change blew slowly here, if at all. The winds of change rustling the leaves of the old magnolia trees and whispering

through the cotton fields was not something most folks were fully ready for.

Mary witnessed the world shifting around her, the lines drawn between the old ways and the new. She saw it in the segregated drinking fountains and the uneasy glances exchanged on Main Street. But she also saw the bravery of those who dared to dream of equality, demanding rights that had been denied.

Her family's porch became a place of heated discussions as evening fell, the fireflies dancing in the twilight. Her father, a quiet man with a deep sense of justice, would talk about Dr. King and the marches. Mary's mother, ever practical, worried about the safety of those pushing for change, yet she never discouraged their aspirations.

As Mary grew, so did her understanding of the complexities of the world. She learned that history was being made not just in far-off cities, but in the very dusty roads she walked every day. The simple joys of childhood remained—the sweet taste of homemade peach cobbler, the thrill of the county fair, the comfort of family and community—but they were now intertwined with a profound awareness of the broader struggles and triumphs shaping their and their neighbors lives.

By the end of the decade, her little town had begun to change, its people tentatively stepping into a new era. And one day, as Mary looked out over the fields she thought about the new fella in her life, a handsome young local boy named... Bobby Harris!

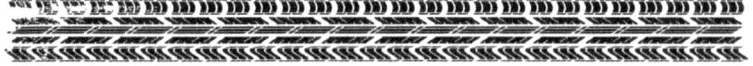

CHAPTER 6

A New Road
A Proper Introduction

"The best way to make a small fortune in racing is to start with a big one."
Darrell Waltrip

The decision to step back from racing was met with mixed reactions in the racing community. Some understood and respected Bobby's choice, while others saw it as a retreat. But for Bobby, it was the right decision. He knew he needed to find a way to stay connected to the sport he loved while also being there for his family.

In the months that followed, Bobby found new ways to channel his passion for racing. He began working as a consultant for other drivers, sharing his knowledge and experience. He also started mentoring young drivers, helping them navigate the challenges of the sport.

Jimmy stayed by his side, their partnership evolving into a business venture. Together, they opened a garage, specializing in building and tuning race cars. It was a way to stay close to the action, to be part of the racing world without the constant danger.

One day, as Bobby and Jimmy were working on a car in the garage, a young man walked in. He was tall and lanky, with a nervous energy about him.

"Excuse me," the young man said, his voice wavering slightly. "Are you Bobby Harris?"

Bobby looked up, wiping his hands on a rag. "I am. What can I do for ya?"

The young man took a deep breath. "My name is

Billy Thompson. I've been racing at local tracks, and I heard you might be able to help me. I want to take my racing to the next level, but I don't know where to start," he said.

Bobby exchanged a glance with Jimmy, a smile tugging at the corners of his mouth. "Well, Billy, you've come to the right place. Let's take a look at what you've got."

Over the next few weeks, Bobby and Jimmy worked closely with Billy, helping him fine-tune his car and improve his driving skills. Bobby saw a lot of potential in the young driver, but he also saw the same fiery determination that had driven him.

As Billy's confidence grew, so did his success on the track. He started winning races, drawing the attention of bigger teams. Bobby felt a sense of satisfaction watching Billy's progress, knowing he had played a part in shaping the young driver's career and future.

One evening, after a particularly successful race, Bobby and Billy sat in the garage, the sounds of crickets filling the night air.

"Damn, you did great out there, Billy," Bobby said, handing him a soda. "You've got what it takes to go far in this sport."

Billy grinned, his eyes shining with excitement. "Thanks, Bobby. I couldn't have done it without you and Jimmy. I owe you guys everything."

Bobby shook his head. "You don't owe us a damn thing. Just remember to stay true to yourself and

never lose sight of why you started racing in the first place."

Billy nodded, a thoughtful expression on his face. "I will, Bobby. I promise."

As Billy left, Bobby leaned back in his chair, a sense of real contentment settling over him. He had found a new purpose, a way to stay connected to the sport he loved while also being there for his family. It wasn't the same as being behind the wheel for sure, but it might be just as fulfilling.

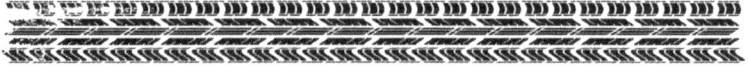

CHAPTER 7

Full Circle
Spiritual not Religious

"When you're racing, there's no time for regret or second-guessing!"
Aj Foyt

Years passed, and Bobby watched with interest as Billy Thompson rose through the ranks, becoming a top driver in the circuit. Bobby's garage became a hub for young drivers seeking guidance, and his reputation as a mentor grew. He found joy in helping others achieve their dreams, knowing he was making a difference.

One sunny afternoon, as Bobby was working on a car in the garage, a familiar voice called out.

"Daddy!" Bobby looked up to see Tommy his son, now a teenager, walking towards him with a wide grin. "Hey, champ! What brings you here?"

Tommy's eyes sparkled with excitement. "I've been thinking, Dad. I want to start racing. I know it's dangerous, but I love it just like you do. Will you teach me?" Bobby felt a surge of emotions— anticipation, fear, excitement. He had always known this day might come, but hearing the words from his son brought it all into focus.

He took a deep breath, looking Tommy in the eye. "If you're sure this is what you want, I'll teach you everything I know. But you have to promise me one thing."

"Anything, Dad," he said.

"Promise me you'll always put *safety* first. Racing is a dangerous sport, and I want you to be careful," Bobby said.

Tommy nodded, his expression serious. "I promise, Dad. I'll be careful."

And so, a new chapter began. Bobby and Tommy spent countless hours at the track, the garage, and in their makeshift classroom at home. Bobby taught

Tommy the fundamentals of racing, the intricacies of car mechanics, and the importance of strategy.

Tommy's first race was a small local event, but to Bobby, it felt monumental. He watched from the sidelines, his heart pounding with a mix of pride and nerves. As the cars lined up and the green flag dropped, Bobby saw the same determination in Tommy's eyes that he had felt all those years ago.

Tommy drove with skill and precision, his natural talent shining through. He navigated the twists and turns of the track with ease, his focus unwavering. When he crossed the finish line in third place, Bobby's heart swelled with pride. It was a solid start, and more importantly, Tommy had raced smart and safe just like his Dad would have..

After the race, Tommy ran over to Bobby, his face flushed with excitement. "Did you see that, Dad? I did it!"

Bobby pulled him into a tight hug, his voice thick with emotion. "You sure did, son. I'm so proud."

Jimmy, who had been watching from the pit, walked over and clapped Tommy on the back. "Not bad for a rookie. Keep listening to your old man, and you'll go far." Bobby's son beamed, his eyes focused with determination. "I will, Uncle Jimmy. I just want to be the very best," Tommy asserted. He was a young man on a mission!

In the months that followed, Tommy continued to improve, racing in more events and honing his skills. Bobby and Jimmy were always there, offering guidance and support. The bond between father and son grew stronger, forged in the heat of competition and the shared love of racing.

But as Tommy's career began to take off, Bobby found himself grappling with conflicting emotions. He was proud of his son's accomplishments, but he couldn't help but worry about the dangers that came with the sport. The memories of crashes and close calls were never far from his mind.

One evening, as they hung out together in the garage, Bobby decided it was time to have a heart-to-heart with his son. "Tommy," Bobby began, his voice serious. "I need to talk to you about something important."

Tommy looked up from the car he was working on, sensing the gravity of his father's tone. "Sure, Dad. What's on your mind?"

Bobby took a deep breath, choosing his words carefully. "You're doing great out there, and I'm incredibly proud of you. But I need you to understand just how dangerous this sport can be. Racing can give you the highest highs, but it can also take everything away in just an instant."

Tommy nodded earnestly. "I know, Dad I know. I've seen the crashes, the injuries. But I love it, just like you did. I promise, I'll be extra careful."

Bobby sighed, reaching out to place a hand on Tommy's shoulder. "I know you will, son. Just remember that there's more to life than racing. Your family, your friends—they're what matter most. Never lose sight of that."

Tommy smiled, his eyes filled with respect and love. "I understand, Dad. And I'll make you a promise... I won't forget."

As Tommy's career progressed, Bobby's worries never fully disappeared, but he took comfort in knowing that his son understood the risks and the importance of safety. And Tommy proved to be a talented and cautious driver, winning races and earning the respect of his peers.

CHAPTER 8

Legacy
A Name Left Behind

"You win some, you lose some, you wreck some!"
Dale Ernhardt Sr.

Years passed, and Bobby watched as Tommy grew and carved out his own legacy in the racing world. He became known for his skill, humor, his sportsmanship, and his dedication to safety. The Harris name continued to be synonymous with excellence on and off the track. The 1960s saw the Harris Racing Team leading in almost all stats.

Bobby and Jimmy's garage flourished as well, becoming a renowned institution in the racing community. They trained and mentored countless young drivers and mechanics, passing on their knowledge and passion for the sport. Bobby's reputation as a mentor grew, and he found fulfillment in helping others achieve their dreams.

One day, as Bobby was working on a car in the garage, a familiar face walked in. It was Billy Thompson, now a seasoned driver and a close friend of the Harris family.

"Hey, Bobby," Billy said grinning. "Got a minute?"

Bobby wiped his hands on a rag and smiled. "For you, always. What brings you by?"

Billy's expression turned serious. "I wanted to talk to you about something. You've done so much for me and for so many others. I think it's time we did something to honor that."

Bobby raised an eyebrow, his curiosity piqued. "What do you have in mind?"

Billy took a deep breath. "I've been talking to some folks in the racing community, and we want to start a scholarship in your name. The Bobby Harris Racing Scholarship, to help young drivers get their start. It's a way to give back and to honor everything you've done for the sport."

Bobby was taken aback, emotion welling up in his chest. "Billy, I don't know what to say. That's... that's incredible."

Billy smiled, his eyes shining with sincerity. "You deserve it, Bobby. You've made a huge impact on so many lives, me included. Just s thank you."

The announcement of the Bobby Harris Racing Scholarship was met with widespread support and enthusiasm. The scholarship provided financial assistance and mentorship to aspiring drivers, giving them the opportunity to pursue their dreams. Bobby took an active role in the program, working closely with the recipients and sharing his wealth of knowledge and experience.

The garage became a hub for the scholarship program, with young drivers coming from all over to learn from Bobby and Jimmy. It was a rewarding and fulfilling endeavor, and Bobby found immense joy in seeing the next generation of racers succeed.

One evening, as Bobby and Mary sat on their porch, watching the sunset, Mary took his hand and smiled.

"You've done so much, Bobby. You've built a legacy that will last for generations."

Bobby squeezed her hand, his heart full. "I couldn't have done it without you, Mary. You've been my rock, my support. I'm just glad I could give back to the sport and help others the way I was helped."

Mary rested her head on his shoulder, a contented sigh escaping her lips. "We've had quite the journey, haven't we?"

Bobby nodded, his eyes reflecting the myriad of memories. "We have. And I wouldn't change a damn thing."

As the years went by, Bobby continued to be a fixture in the racing community. He attended races, mentored drivers, and remained involved in the scholarship program. Tommy's career flourished, and he eventually became a champion driver, fulfilling his own dreams and carrying on the famous Harris racing legacy.

Bobby watched with pride as his son achieved greatness, knowing that he had played a part in shaping his journey. And through it all, he never lost sight of what mattered most—his family, his friends, and the love and support that had carried him through every challenge.

CHAPTER 9

The Final Lap
Time Flies

"What's behind you doesn't matter."
Enzo Ferrari

As Bobby entered his twilight years, he reflected on the incredible journey that had brought him to this point. He had faced challenges, celebrated victories, and built a life filled with love, family, and a deep connection to the sport he adored.

One sunny afternoon, Bobby decided to take a drive to the old dirt track where it had all begun. He hadn't been there in years, but he felt a strong pull to revisit the place that had sparked his passion for racing. He arrived at the track, the dusty road and weathered grandstands evoking a flood of memories. Bobby parked his truck and walked slowly towards the stands, each step a reminder of the countless laps, the victories and defeats, the friends he had made and lost.

As he sat down on one of the old wooden benches, Bobby felt a profound sense of peace. He had come full circle, returning to the place where it all began, a testament to a life well-lived and a legacy that would endure. Mary, somehow sensing where Bobby had gone, joined him at the track. She sat beside him, their hands intertwined, the bond between them stronger than ever.

"It's been quite a ride, hasn't it?" Mary said, her voice filled with love and nostalgia.

Bobby nodded, his eyes misty with emotion. "It has. And I wouldn't trade it for anything."

They sat in comfortable silence, the memories of their shared journey filling the space between them. The sun began to dip below the horizon, casting a golden glow over the track. The memories flowed like a river—each race, each challenge, each victory, and every moment of heartache and joy that had defined their lives.

"I remember the first time I saw you race," Mary said softly, her eyes sparkling. "You were so full of fire and determination. I knew then that you were destined for greatness."

Bobby chuckled, a warm smile spreading across his face. "And I remember seeing you in the stands, cheering louder than anyone else. You've always been my biggest fan, Mary."

Mary leaned her head on his shoulder, a contented sigh escaping her lips. "We've had our ups and downs, but I wouldn't change a thing. We've built something beautiful together, Bobby."

Bobby nodded, a lump forming in his throat. "We have. And I'm so grateful for every moment."

As they sat there, reminiscing, the sound of an engine roared in the distance. Tommy had arrived, to do more training. He drove onto the track, his car gleaming in the fading light. He parked near the stands and walked over, his eyes filled with respect and admiration.

"Hey, Dad," Tommy said, his voice tinged with emotion. "Thought I might find ya here."

Bobby smiled, standing up to embrace his only son. "Just taking a trip down old memory lane. It's good to see you son!"

Tommy joined them on the bench, the three of

them sitting together, a family united by love and a shared passion for racing.

"I've been thinking a lot about everything you've taught me," Tommy said, his voice thoughtful. "Not just about racing, but about life. You've shown me what it means to follow your dreams, to work hard, and to always put family first. I hope I can live up to that legacy."

Bobby placed a hand on Tommy's shoulder, his eyes shining with pride. "You already have, son. You've made me prouder than I can put into words. And I know you'll continue to make a difference, both on and off the track."

The three of them sat in silence, watching as the last rays of sunlight painted the sky in hues of pink and orange. It was a moment of pure serenity, a fitting tribute to the racing journey they had shared together over the years.

CHAPTER 10

Tomorrow
A Lasting Racing Legacy

"Lead, follow or get the hell outta the way!"
Bobby Harris

Years later, the Bobby Harris Racing Team and its innovative scholarship program had grown into one of the most respected in the racing world. Many of its recipients had gone on to become successful drivers or mechanics, crediting Bobby's mentorship and the support of the program for their achievements.

The garage, now run by Tommy, had become a beacon for aspiring racers. It was a place where dreams were nurtured, and young drivers learned not just about racing, but about integrity, hard work, and the importance of family. Tommy continued to honor his father's legacy, ensuring that the values Bobby had instilled remained at the heart of everything they did.

Bobby and Mary enjoyed their retirement, spending their days surrounded by family and friends. They often visited the garage, offering wisdom and encouragement to the young drivers. Bobby found immense joy in watching the next generation take to the track, knowing that he had played a small part in their journey to try and reach victory lane.

One summer day, the racing community gathered at the garage to celebrate Bobby's life and legacy. It was a joyous occasion, filled with laughter, stories, and heartfelt tributes. Drivers, both young and old, spoke about the impact Bobby had on their lives, sharing memories of his guidance, kindness, and unwavering support.

As the sun set, casting a golden glow over the garage, Bobby stood up to address the crowd. He looked out at the sea of faces, many of them familiar, and felt a deep sense of fulfillment.

"Thanks for being here," Bobby began, his voice steady and strong. "It means the world to me to see so many friends and family gathered together. Racing has always been more than just a sport to me. It's a way of life, a community, and a family."
He paused, his eyes scanning the crowd. "I've been incredibly fortunate to have had the support of so

many amazing people. From Mary, who has been my rock, to Jimmy, my partner in crime, to all the young drivers who have passed through these doors. You've all made this journey worthwhile."

Bobby took a deep breath, his voice filled with emotion. "I'm proud of what we've built here, and I know that the future is bright. To all the young drivers out there, keep pushing, keep dreaming, and never forget the importance of family and integrity. That's the true heart of racing." The crowd erupted in applause, and Bobby felt a wave of gratitude wash over him. As the celebration continued, he stood with Mary and Tommy, watching as the next generation of racers mingled, shared stories, and talked about the future.

In the twilight of his life, Bobby Harris knew that he had left a lasting legacy. It was a legacy of passion, perseverance, and the enduring power of family. And as he looked at the faces around him, he knew

that his spirit would live on in the hearts of those who carried the torch forward.

For Bobby and Tommy, the journey had come full circle. Both had started as young men with a dream, faced countless challenges, and emerged as a beloved figure in the racing community. Their stories were ones of triumph and persistence, and will continue to inspire generations to come. And as he rounded the 4th turn of the race track Bobby Harris smiled, knowing that he'd lived a life filled with purpose, and a passion for racing that had driven him every step of the way.

CHAPTER 11

Passing the Torch
Building on Youth

*"If you're in control, you're not
going fast enough."*
Parnelli Jones

As Bobby grew older, he began to think about the future of the garage and the legacy he had built. He knew that one day he would need to pass the torch to the next generation, and he wanted to ensure that everything he had worked for would continue to not only survive but thrive.

One crisp autumn afternoon, as Bobby and Jimmy were working in the garage, Tommy walked in, now a seasoned driver with a wealth of experience under his belt and a little swagger to go with it.

"Dad, Uncle Jimmy," Tommy began, his tone more serious. "I've been thinking about the future. You've built something incredible here, and I want to make sure it all continues."

Bobby looked up, a sense of pride swelling in his chest. "What do you have in mind, Tommy? I know you can do anything you put your mind too."

Tommy took a deep breath. "I want to take on a bigger role in the garage. I've learned so much from you both, and I think I'm ready to help run things. I want to keep the legacy alive and make sure the scholarship program continues to grow."

Jimmy nodded, a smile spreading across his face. "Sounds like a plan to me. What do you think, Bobby? You think the kid is ready?"

Bobby felt a mix of emotions—achievement, nostalgia, and a sense of fulfillment. He knew that Tommy was ready, and he couldn't think of a better person to carry on the legacy.

"I think it's a great idea," Bobby said, his voice filled with warmth. "You've got my full support, Tommy. And I know you'll do an incredible job."

With Tommy taking on a leadership role, the garage continued to flourish. He brought new ideas and energy, while also respecting the traditions and values that Bobby and Jimmy had instilled. The scholarship program expanded, reaching even more aspiring drivers and providing them with the resources and mentorship they needed to succeed.

Bobby and Jimmy took a step back, allowing Tommy to take the reins, but they remained involved, offering guidance and support whenever needed. It was a new chapter for the garage, and Bobby felt a deep sense of satisfaction knowing that the legacy he had built was in good hands.

The years had passed… and as if ordained by the racing gods, Bobby fittingly died at Talladega Raceway in a 'Old Timers' race after hitting the 4th turn wall at approximately 100mph and leaving Mary and Tommy to continue the Harris racing legacy. Most felt like it was destiny that Bobby passed there and like that... and no one who really knew him was surprised. Besides Tommy would continue. And he did.

The Darlington Raceway, is known as 'The Lady in Black,' and is the heart of stock car racing... always had been. Its asphalt curves gleam under the relentless sun, a challenge for any driver brave enough to face its infamous "Too Tough to Tame" moniker. On race day, the grandstands fill with a motley assembly: local farmers in their dusty overalls, well-to-do businessmen in pressed slacks and button-down shirts, and the ever-present contingent of gear heads, their hands perpetually stained with grease and oil.

Tommy 'Tomcat' Harris was one such gearhead. At 26, he was neither a rookie nor a seasoned veteran. He was caught in that middle ground where dreams of glory were just within reach, but financial reality was a constant companion. His father, Bobby Harris, had been a racing legend in his own right, his name still spoken with reverence in hushed tones in garages across the South. The old man had passed on after a spectacular crash at Talladega, but Bobby's shadow still loomed large over his son Tommy and the racing community.

Tommy's car, a 1964 Chevy Impala, gleamed a deep blue under the harsh sunlight, its number 43 painted in bold white on the side. It was a beauty, lovingly maintained and modified, its roar a familiar sound in the Harris garage. Tommy's best friend and chief mechanic, Jeb Stuart, leaned over the engine, his brow furrowed in concentration. Jeb had a knack for coaxing every last bit of horsepower out of an engine, a skill honed through years of trial and error.

"You reckon she's ready, Jeb?" Tommy asked, wiping his hands on a rag as he approached.

Jeb straightened up, a smirk playing at the corners of his mouth. "Damn straight! She's purrin' like a kitten, Tomcat. Just you wait and see. You're gonna give 'em hell out there today!"

Tommy nodded, feeling a mix of excitement and anxiety knot in his stomach. Race days always did this to him, the anticipation building until the moment the flag dropped and everything else faded away. He climbed into the Impala, the interior smelling of gasoline and sweat, and fired up the engine. The car growled to life, vibrating with pent-up power.

The grandstands buzzed with energy as the race drew closer. Vendors hawked hot dogs and cold beers, the scents mingling with the tang of motor oil and exhaust. Children ran between the legs of adults, their laughter a bright counterpoint to the gruff conversations of their elders.

Among the crowd was Peggy, Tommy's girlfriend, her auburn hair tied back in a ponytail, a faded red bandana holding it in place. She wore a simple white blouse and jeans, but to Tommy, she was the most beautiful woman in the world. She stood with Tommy's mother, Mary, a stoic woman who had seen her husband and now her son take on the dangerous world of racing.

"Think he'll do good today?" Peggy, Tommy's girlfriend, asked, her voice tinged with worry.
Mary nodded, her gaze steady on the track. "He's got the Harris blood. And that boy's got a fire in him, just like his Daddy had. He'll be fine."

Tommy guided the Impala into the starting line-up, his heart pounding in sync with the rumble of engines around him. He glanced to his right and saw Jimmy 'The Bullet' Johnson in his bright red Ford Galaxy, a cocky grin plastered on his face. He was a fierce competitor, known for his aggressive driving and doing whatever it takes to win.

The announcer's voice boomed over the loudspeakers, building the excitement to a fever pitch. "Ladies and gentlemen, welcome to the darling of the Southland, Darlington Raceway! Get ready for the one and only... Southern 500!"

As the cars began their pace laps, Tommy took a deep breath, focusing his mind. This was it. This was what he lived for. The flag dropped, and the roar of engines filled the air as the cars surged forward, tires screeching against the asphalt and began their dance of danger.

The first few laps were a blur of speed and noise. Tommy settled into a rhythm, his hands steady on the wheel, eyes scanning the track for openings. He knew every inch of this course, every bump and curve. It was a dance of danger, where one wrong move could end in disaster.

As the laps wore on, the field began to thin out, the weaker cars falling behind or succumbing to mechanical failures. Tommy pushed the Impala harder, inching his way up the ranks. He could feel the car responding to his every command, Jeb's meticulous tuning paying off.

Halfway through the race, disaster struck. A multi-car pileup in Turn Three sent metal and rubber flying. Tommy swerved to avoid the wreckage, narrowly missing a spinning car. His heart pounded in his chest as he navigated through the debris, grateful for Jeb's insistence on reinforcing the Impala's chassis.

The caution flag came out, and the pace slowed as the track was cleared. Tommy used the opportunity to catch his breath and assess his position. He was in the top five, a good spot but not good enough. He needed to push harder, take more risks.

The green flag waved, and the race resumed. Tommy felt a surge of adrenaline as he gunned the engine, the Impala leaping forward with renewed vigor. He was in the zone now, the world outside the track fading into insignificance. It was just him, the car, and the race.

He fought his way past car after car, his skill and determination evident in every maneuver. The crowd roared as he closed in on the leaders, their cheers a distant echo in his mind. He could see Jimmy Johnson up ahead, the red Galaxy 500 a tantalizing target that was hard to miss.

With ten laps to go, Tommy made his move. He darted to the inside on a tight corner, the Impala hugging the asphalt as he drew alongside Jimmy. The two cars raced side by side, inches apart, neither willing to give an inch.

Jimmy glanced over, his grin replaced by a look of grim determination. Tommy could feel the tension, the unspoken challenge between them. It was a battle of wills, a test of who wanted it more.

In the final lap, they were neck and neck. The crowd was on its feet, the noise deafening. Tommy could feel the Impala straining, every part of it pushing to the limit. He took a deep breath, focusing all his energy on the finish line.

As they roared into the final turn, Tommy saw his chance. He nudged the Impala forward, just enough to edge ahead. Jimmy tried to counter, but it was too

late. With a final burst of speed, Tommy crossed the finish line, the checkered flag waving triumphantly.

The noise of the crowd washed over Tommy as he slowed the Impala to a stop. He sat for a moment, letting the reality of his victory sink in. He had done it. He had won the Southern 500! If on his Dad could have lived long enough to see it. But he chose to believe that Bobby Harris was looking down on him from heaven and was very pleased.

Climbing out of the car, he was met by Jeb, his face split by a wide grin. "I knew you could do it, Tomcat!" he shouted, slapping Tommy on the back. Tommy laughed, the adrenaline still coursing through his veins. He looked up to see Peggy running towards him, her face alight with joy. She threw her arms around him, and he held her close, the world a blur of color and sound.

His mother approached, her eyes shining with pride. "Your daddy would be so proud," she said softly, and Tommy felt a lump in his throat.

The trophy presentation was a blur, the weight of the cup solid and reassuring in his hands. As he stood on the podium, he looked out over the crowd, feeling a sense of accomplishment and belonging. This was his world, his passion, and he'd been found worthy.

In the days that followed, Tommy became a local hero. Newspapers ran stories about his victory, and people he barely knew congratulated him on the street. But he knew that the world of stock car racing was fickle. Today's hero could be tomorrow's forgotten name.

He spent hours in the garage with Jeb, tweaking and tuning the Impala, preparing for the next race. The Southern 500 was a significant victory, but it was just one race. There were always more challenges ahead, more races to win.

One evening, as the sun dipped below the horizon, Tommy and Jeb sat on the porch of the Garrison home, cold beers in hand. The cicadas sang their twilight song, and the air was thick with the scent of summer in the southland.

"What's next for you, Tomcat?" Jeb asked, his eyes reflecting the fading light.

Tommy took a long pull from his beer, considering the question. "Keep racing, keep winning. Maybe one day, I'll be as good as the old man."

Jeb nodded, a knowing smile on his lips. "You're already well on your way, my friend."

As the stars began to twinkle in the night sky, Tommy felt a deep sense of contentment. He had a long road ahead, full of challenges and uncertainties, but he had a solid foundation and was ready to make his Daddy proud.

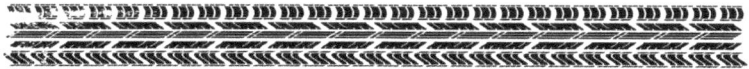

FAST FACTS

Here are some facts about NASCAR, or the National Association for Stock Car Auto Racing:

NASCAR's first race was held in 1948 at Daytona Beach's beach road course, and Red Byron won in a Ford. NASCAR has only had two seasons without a road race, in 1959 and 1962.

The only sport in the United States with more fans than NASCAR is professional NFL football

NASCAR drivers compete on four types of tracks: short tracks, intermediate ovals, superspeedways, and road courses. Up to 40 cars may participate in a Cup Series race. The Daytona 500, also known as "The Great American Race", is considered one of the most iconic events of the NASCAR season.

Drivers are not required to have a driver's license. They must, however, pass drug screens and physicals and be thoroughly vetted before being allowed to compete.

Each year, NASCAR sanctions over 1,500 races at over 100 tracks in 48 US states, as well as in Canada, Mexico, Brazil and Europe

Employing more than 5000 people NASCAR is

considered one of the world's top motorsports organizations and one of America's most popular spectator sports will millions of fans attending races across America each year.

The name originally chosen for the series was National Stock Car Racing Association; when it was pointed out that that name was already in use by a rival sanctioning body, "National Association for Stock Car Auto Racing", proposed by mechanic Red Vogt, was selected as the organization's name.

A NASCAR race team will wear out over 15 sets of tires a race series.

The temperature in a NASCAR car can reach 170 degrees. Drivers experience between two and three G's when making turns on the track. This is equal to up to three times the force of gravity.

Richard Petty won the Daytona 500 seven times and is widely regarded as the best driver of all time, but most fans don't know that Petty also invented the Window Net that is used on race cars? It helps to prevent injuries by keeping a driver's arms inside the car in the event of a crash.

CHAPTER 12

Now A Word From Our Sponsors
Corporate Support = Success

"Money makes the wheels go around!"
Bobby Unser

Bobby sat in his trailer, the low hum of the racetrack vibrating through the walls. Outside, the roar of engines was a constant reminder of the high stakes that defined his world. He took a deep breath, glancing at the schedule on his pad. Every second was accounted for, every detail meticulously planned, not a moment to waste. This was the life of a professional race car driver.

He rubbed his temples, feeling the weight of expectations pressing down on him. His sponsors' logos plastered on every inch of his race suit and car weren't just for show; they were a constant reminder of the hundreds of thousands of dollars (soon to be millions) riding on his performance. Each corporate logo decal represented a contract, set of deliverables, and a promise of return on investment (ROI). Bobby's career wasn't just about speed and skill—it was now a business, and he was the product. There was a lot at stake from millions of dollars in ad revenues to jobs to reputations.

Under the glaring lights of the stadium, the pit crew bustled around the cars, a hive of activity that masked the intricate web of commerce driving the spectacle. Stock car sponsorships were not merely about branding; they were complex alliances, where corporate giants invested in speed and spectacle to capture the hearts and wallets of fans.

Sponsorship deals were sometimes as cutthroat as the races themselves. Behind the scenes, suits in boardrooms debated his worth based on metrics, and viewer ratings. To them, Bobby was just a brand, a marketable asset able to deliver 'eyeballs' to view their logos. To Bobby, the pressure was suffocating. Every race, every turn, every pit stop was scrutinized, analyzed, and judged. A single mistake could cost him more than just the race—it could cost him money and ultimately his career.

His primary sponsor, a multinational oil corporation, had invested heavily in him this season. Their CEO, Mr. Chambers, had made it clear during their last meeting: "We expect results, Bobby. We're putting millions into this partnership. We need you to perform and deliver."

"*Perform.*" The word echoed in Bobby's mind. It wasn't just about winning; it was about being the face of the brand, engaging with fans, and maintaining a pristine public image. It was about the high-stakes PR game where one slip-up could lead to a cascade of lost endorsements and plummeting stock prices. The financial implications were staggering, and the pressure was immense. But Bobby thrived on the edge. The thrill of the race, the adrenaline coursing through his veins, the blur of the track as he pushed his car to the limits—these were the moments he lived for. Yet, as exhilarating as it all was, the reality was always there, lurking in the background. The meetings, the press conferences, the constant scrutiny—it was a delicate balance between passion and performance.

He stood up, stretching his arms, trying to shake off the tension. Outside, the sun was setting, casting a golden hue over the track. Tomorrow was another race, another chance to prove himself. He knew his sponsors would be watching, their eyes on every move he made, every second he shaved off his time. Bobby was ready. He had to be. In this world, there was no room for anything less than true perfection.

That night, sleep was again elusive. The noise from the pit crew working late, the constant ringing of his phone with messages from his manager, and the ever-present thoughts of strategies and techniques kept him awake. Mr. Chambers words echoed in his head. "Don't let us down, Bobby. We believe in you." The words felt like a double-edged sword—supportive yet heavy with expectation.

Morning came too soon, the dawn light piercing through the thin curtains of the trailer. Bobby rolled out of bed, his body stiff but his mind sharp. He went through his routine with mechanical precision: a quick workout, a healthy high protein breakfast, and then a final review of the race plan with his team. Every detail mattered and every second counted both in the pits and on the track.

In the garage, his car gleamed under the fluorescent lights. It was a true marvel of engineering, a testament to the skill and dedication of the crew that had built it. He ran his hand along the sleek surface, feeling the power contained within. The corporate logos of his sponsors stood out boldly against the metallic paint, each one a silent partner in his quest for victory lane.

As he suited up, Bobby felt a surge of determination. He knew that beyond the track, in corporate offices and living rooms around the world, people were watching. They had placed their bets on him, invested their money and trust. It was a heavy burden, but also a source of strength. He was not just racing for himself; he was racing for all those who believed in him.

Walking to the starting line, the cacophony of the crowd hit him like a wave. The air was electric with anticipation. He climbed into the cockpit, the familiar confines of the car enveloping him. The countdown began, and with each passing second, the world outside faded away. It was just him and the machine, man and metal, who along with his logos was ready to face the challenge ahead.

The green light flashed, and Bobby launched forward, the engine roaring to life. The track blurred beneath him, the world reduced to a series of high-speed calculations and instinctual reactions. Every turn, every acceleration, was a test of his skill and his nerve. He always passed the test!

The pressure was immense, but Bobby thrived on it. He pushed harder, faster, determined to leave nothing on the table. Lap after lap, he battled not just the other drivers but also the expectations weighing on his shoulders. The race was a blur of speed and strategy, each decision critical. And then, in a heartbeat, it was over. He crossed the finish line, heart pounding, adrenaline coursing through his veins and all the while the oil company logo was the visual priority. They made sure of that.

As the car coasted to a stop, Bobby removed his helmet, feeling the cool air against his sweat-soaked face. The crowd erupted in cheers, and he knew he had delivered. For today, at least, he had met the expectations of fans and sponsors. The weight lifted slightly, but he knew it would return. The life of a professional driver was a cycle of proving oneself, of living up to the promises made to sponsors.

He climbed out of the car, raising his arms in triumph. The cameras flashed, capturing the moment and the logos that covered his race suit. But even as he basked in the glory, Bobby knew that tomorrow the pressure would start anew. It takes money to race and in this high-stakes world of racing sponsorships, there is no time to rest because every victory hopefully means more sales for the sponsors.

At the next race Bobby again stood by his car, watching as his crew adjusted the decals that covered nearly every inch of the vehicle. Each sticker represented hours of negotiations and millions of dollars. The logos weren't just advertisements; they were statements of faith from companies betting on the symbiotic relationship between success on the track and their profits.

Another new sponsorship from Falcon Electronics was the biggest coup. Their CEO, Janet Reeves, was a hard-nosed businesswoman with a keen eye for opportunity. At their last meeting in her sleek, glass-walled office, she had made her expectations crystal clear. "We're not just investing in your car, Bobby. We're investing in you. Every race, every interview, every public appearance—you're

representing Falcon. Please remember that." He nodded, understanding the weight of her words. Falcon's investment was massive, enough to ensure his team had the best equipment, the best training. But in return, they wanted results. Their faith in him was measured in ROI, brand visibility, and market penetration.

Other sponsors followed suit, drawn to the magnetic pull of Bobby's rising star. From energy drinks to automotive parts, each company saw a chance to align their brand with the excitement and glamour of racing... of winning. Mountain Roar Energy Drinks had splashed their vibrant logo across the hood, betting that the sight of Bobby's car crossing the finish line first would translate to millions of cans flying off the shelves.

In the paddock, Bobby could see representatives from these companies mingling, their sharp suits a stark contrast to the grease-streaked overalls of the pit crew. They were here to watch their investment in action, to see if their calculated risk would pay off in the form of trophies and televised triumphs. Each of them had their own metrics of success— TV ratings, product sales spikes—and Bobby was at the center of it all. He liked that.

The pressure was continual. Every sponsor had a story, a set of expectations that went beyond the track. Apex Motors, another major backer, had sent over a film crew to document behind the scenes at the race, creating content for their marketing campaigns and commercials.

"Authenticity sells," the director had said, adjusting the lighting to capture the sweat on Bobby's brow. "We want to show the real you—the dedication, the drive. That's what really resonates with people, with the fans."

Bobby smiled for the camera, though the weight of those words pressed down on him. Authenticity, dedication, drive—these weren't just traits; they were commodities, packaged and sold in the form of glossy advertisements and inspiring customer enthusiasm and loyalty.

As the race day unfolded, the sponsors watched with bated breath. Bobby could feel their eyes on him, their hopes pinned on his performance. He knew that every lap was not just a chance to win but a demonstration of value for the brands that had tied their fortunes to his. The roar of the crowd was matched by the silent calculations of marketing executives, each moment on the track a potential advertising pitch meeting or a video highlight reel for future negotiations.

Later, in the relative quiet of his trailer, Bobby reflected on the nature of his racing partnerships. These companies weren't just funding his career;

they were integral to it. Their investments allowed him to compete at the highest level, but they also demanded a piece of his success. It was a delicate balance, a high-wire act where one misstep could send everything tumbling.

As he peeled off his racing suit, he caught sight of the logos again, each one a reminder of the intricate dance between sport and commerce. In the world of modern stock car racing, speed and skill were paramount, but so too were the relationships forged in boardrooms and broadcasted to millions. Bobby understood that as long as he could deliver both on and off the track, the financial wheels would keep turning, the sponsors would keep investing, and his dreams and team would remain intact.

HARRIS

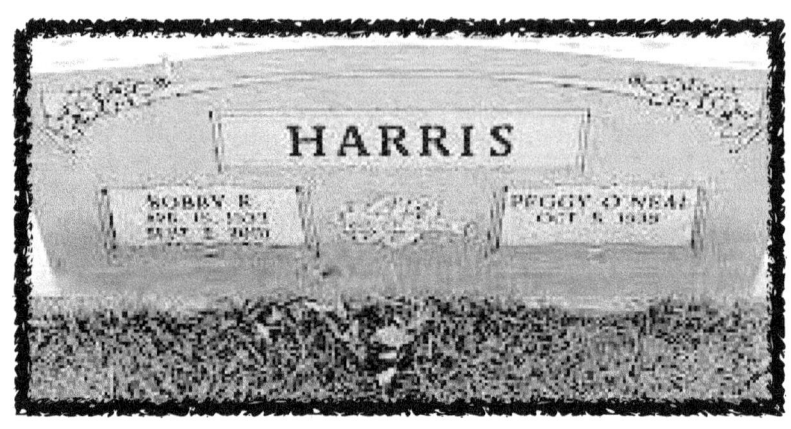

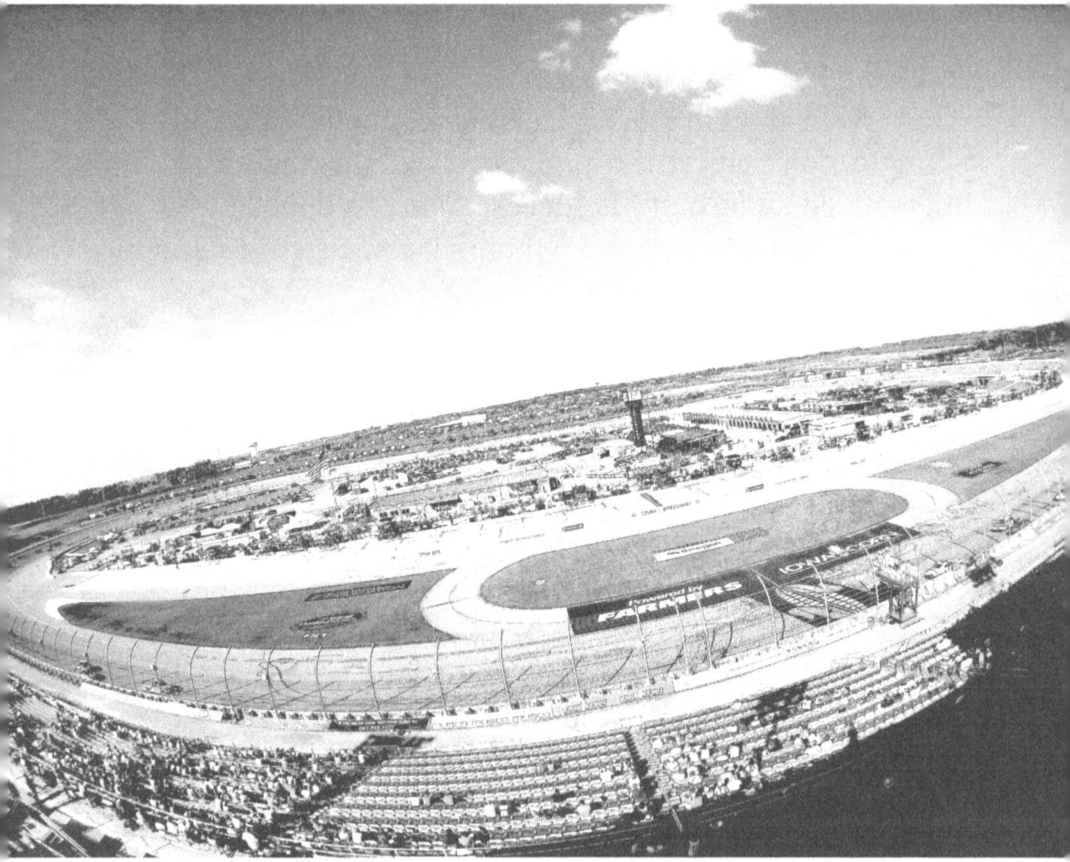
Powered by
FARMERS

Chapter 13

And in the End
A Fitting Finish

"The winner is the one who refuses to lose!"
Dale Earnhardt

It had been 10 years but memories of Bobby and his passing often came flashing back for Mary and her son. They remembered every moment of that fateful day. It was a typical blue sky race day and the roar of race engines reverberated through Talladega Super Speedway, a cacophony of horsepower and steel. The sun hung high, casting stark shadows over the track, its relentless glare almost as intense as the tension palpable in the air. Bobby "Hot Shoe" Harris, known for his fearless driving and winning smile, was again in the thick of it, his stock car a blur of colors as it hurtled through the turns and down the straightaway.

Lap after lap, Bobby's car danced on the edge of control, tires skimming the outer limits of traction. The crowd roared with every maneuver, every daring pass, their cheers merging into a singular, deafening wave. Inside his helmet, the world was narrowed to the roar of his engine, the vibration through the wheel, and the rhythmic pounding of his heart... that and the track before him.

Coming out of Turn 3, Bobby felt a surge of adrenaline. He was in the zone, the car responding to his every command with the precision of a scalpel. Turn 4 loomed ahead, a wide arc that promised glory or disaster. He shifted his weight, adjusting for the perfect entry. But as he initiated the turn, something felt wrong. A slight tremor, almost imperceptible, but enough to send a chill down his spine. In a fraction of a second, it became clear: a tire had blown. The car wobbled, then skidded, tires screeching in protest. Bobby grabbed the wheel and regained control, but the forces were too great.

The car spun, a blur of color and motion, then slammed into the wall. The impact was brutal, metal crumpling like paper, sparks flying as the vehicle disintegrated against the barrier. For a moment, there was only silence, the world holding its breath. Then the flames erupted, licking hungrily at the wreckage.Emergency crews scrambled, their movements a frantic blur. The crowd's roar had turned to gasps, then hushed whispers, a collective exhalation of fear and disbelief. In the control tower, voices crackled over radios, the urgency unmistakable.

But within the cocoon of his mangled car, Bobby was gone. The fearless driver who had once danced on the razor's edge between life and death had finally tipped over. His last moments, a symphony of speed and terror, were etched into the annals of Talladega's storied history.

As the sun began to set, casting long shadows over the track, the world mourned the loss of Bobby "Hot Shoe" Harris. In the pits, fellow drivers removed their helmets, heads bowed in silent tribute. The stands, once a sea of motion and noise, stood still, a quiet testament to the fragility of life and the relentless pursuit of glory that defined it. And somewhere beyond the horizon, the echoes of that fateful day would linger, a haunting reminder of the price sometimes paid in the pursuit of speed.

Mary Harris clutched the railing of the VIP box, her knuckles white against the metal. Her heart pounding in her chest as she watched Bobby's car tear through the track. Every race was a fresh onslaught of anxiety, but today, something felt different, ominous. Her eyes, usually bright and full of life, were now shadowed with worry, following the blur of red and white as it sped around Talladega's high banked curves.

Next to her, Tommy Harris stood on tiptoes, trying to get a better view. He was the spitting image of Bobby—dark hair, piercing blue eyes, and an infectious smile that could light up a room. His hero, his dad, was out there doing what he did best. Tommy wore a miniature version of Bobby's racing jacket, a birthday gift from his father. Today, he clutched a toy car, a perfect replica of Bobby's stock car, his fingers tracing the familiar contours absentmindedly.

As Bobby entered Turn 4, time seemed to stand still. Mary's breath caught in her throat as she noticed the subtle wobble of the race car, the hint of something had gone terribly wrong. She barely had time to react before the car veered, spun out of control, and collided with the wall. The impact was immediate and violent, a crescendo of sound and fury that seemed to freeze the world around her.

Mary's scream was swallowed by the cacophony, her hand flying to her mouth. Beside her, Tommy's eyes widened in shock, the toy car slipping from his grasp and clattering to the floor. He stared at the track, disbelief and terror written on his young face.

"Mom, what's happening? Is Dad okay?" Tommy's voice was a thin whisper, trembling with fear.
Mary's heart shattered at the sound of her son's voice. She wanted to reassure him, to tell him that everything would be alright, but the words stuck in her throat. She could only watch, helpless, as the emergency crews descended on the scene, their movements frantic and purposeful.

Tears streamed down Mary's face, her vision blurring as she clung to Tommy. She held him close, feeling his small body shaking against hers."I don't know, sweetheart. I don't know," she whispered, her voice breaking.

Minutes felt like hours as they waited for news. The spectators' hushed murmurs filled the air, a stark contrast to the roaring excitement of just moments

before. Mary prayed silently, her thoughts a jumble of fear and hope.

When the grim news finally came, it was delivered with a somberness that left no room for doubt. Bobby "Hot Shoe" Harris, the man she had loved with every fiber of her being, was gone. The reality hit her like a physical blow, and she staggered, her legs threatening to give way beneath her.

Tommy looked up at her, tears streaming down his cheeks. "Mom, is Dad...?" Mary nodded, unable to speak, her heart breaking anew at the sight of her son's devastation. She pulled him close, wrapping him in a fierce embrace, as the reality of their loss settled over them both. It was a sad time.

In the stands, surrounded by the echoes of cheers the crowd turned to sorrow, Mary and Tommy held onto each other, united in their grief and love for the man who had lived life on the edge, and paid the ultimate price for his passion.

In the end, the race, like his life, was a blur of speed and strategy, of wins and loses, another testament to the teamwork and technology that sponsorships had made possible. When Bobby crossed the final finish line in heaven, the faint cheers of the crowd mingled with the reserved applause from the corporate suite over the years and filled his ears and he knew the end was here.

He had delivered on the skills God had given him and as he faded from this life with loving thoughts of Mary, Tommy and his pit crew... he knew the cycle would somehow start anew with the next race and driver and with the thought of that and with his last breath... he smiled.

The Anatomy of a Stock Car

As the saying goes, *'there's nothing stock about a stock car!'* A type of automobile specifically modified for racing, typically on oval tracks or dirt. Originating from standard production models available to the public, these cars undergo extensive modifications to enhance performance, safety, and durability for competitive racing.

Key Features:

1. <u>Chassis and Body</u>: The chassis is often custom-built for strength and rigidity, while the body is designed to resemble a production car but optimized for aerodynamics. The outer shell might be made of lightweight materials like fiberglass or sheet metal.

2. <u>Engine</u>: High-performance engines are a hallmark, often V8s in American stock car racing, producing significant horsepower. These engines are finely tuned for maximum speed and acceleration.

3. <u>Suspension and Tires</u>: Racing suspensions are installed for better handling and stability. Tires are

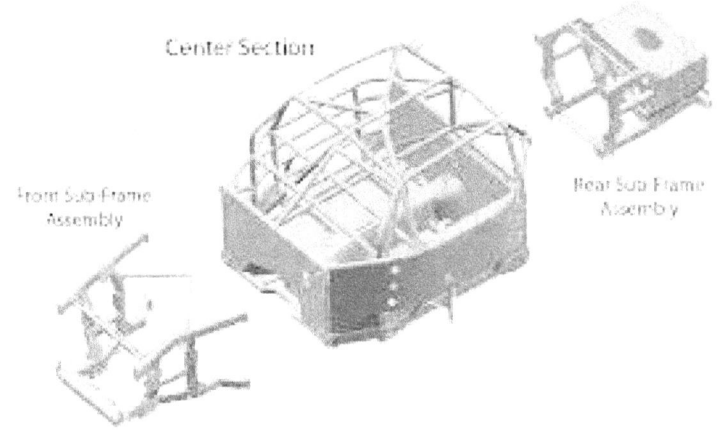

Center Section

Front Sub-Frame
Assembly

Rear Sub-Frame
Assembly

specialized for different track conditions, offering maximum grip and durability.

4. Safety Features: Roll cages, reinforced frames, fuel cells, and fire suppression systems are critical for driver safety. The cars also have safety harnesses, helmets, and HANS (Head and Neck Support) devices for driver protection.

5. Interior: The interior is stripped of non-essential components to reduce weight, featuring only necessary gauges, a racing seat, and controls.

Key Parts:
The Roll Cage
The part of the frame with the thickest tubing. It's designed to keep drivers safe in all accidents.

The Front Clip
Made of thinner material than the roll cage. It is

designed to collapse on impact, and push the engine out of the bottom of the car to avoid the driver completely. The Rear Clip is lso designed to be collapsible and absorbs the most of it on the event of an accident.

The Firewall

A metal panel with fire retardant materials placed in the frame that separates the driver's compartment from the engine compartment.

Aerodynamics

One of the main goals in body design is to reduce drag. NASCAR has designed 30 different templates that determine the shape of the body of the car. The body is mounted forward on the frame, the sides and fenders are less contoured. The grill opening is tested thoroughly in a wind tunnel.

Engine Minimums

NASCAR engines have to produce a vast amount of power, up to 750 HP steadily for 3.5 – 4.5 hours without turbochargers, superchargers and the like.
Some stock cars have restrictor plates that reduce engine horsepower from 750HP to 450HP.

Tire Regulations

NASCAR tires have to remain stable in very high temperatures and at high speeds. They must provide unparalleled traction and be changeable during a pit stop in 12 to 14 seconds!

Weight

A NASCAR car has weight requirements of 3,200 lbs (1,451 kg) minimum without driver and fuel 3,400 lb (1,542 kg) minimum with driver and fuel.

Fuel

Stock cars use 'Sunoco Green E15', a high-octane, unleaded fuel blend that's 15% ethanol and has an octane rating of 98. The fuel is green in color, which is how it got its name. With 18 gallon fuel tanks cars typically use 100 gallons of fuel in a 500-mile race, getting about 5 miles per gallon.

Stock cars are synonymous with race series where they compete on tracks varying from high banked Super speedways to short ovals to dirt tracks to road courses, all providing a unique blend of speed and tactical racing. Stock cars may superficially resemble your family sedan but they're in fact hi-tech racing machines built to a strict set of regulations ensuring that the chassis, suspension, engine, etc. are, *from an engineering and competition standpoint,* as identical as possible.

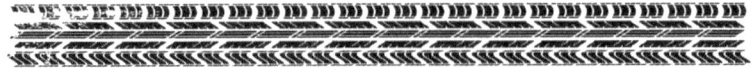

Credits & Acknowledgments

NASCAR, USRA, HSCRA, FASCAR, NSA, ASCA

AP Photos and other used by permission

Tim Bryant, Five Flags Speedway, Pensacola, FL

Some Images licensed by DepositPhotos.com

Some Photography by Tom McAuliffe

Jeremy Austin, Driver/Race Team Owner

Action Sports Photography Inc.

Bob McDonald, NASCAR Media Relations

Gearhead Advisor Thad Tinney

Professor Dale Evans

Draft 2 Digital Publishing

Southern Raceway, Milton, FL

Turner Sports Corp. (TNT)

Blake Harris, Hendrick Motorsports

The Motor Racing Network

Northwest Florida Speedway

The Harvill Foundation

The Racing Experience, Atlanta Speedway, GA

Editor Nevvie Gane - *www.nevviegane.com*

> W E B   S I T E S <

https://www.nascar.com/
https://www.stockcarracefans.com/
www.SprintCarFan.com
https://vscracing.com/
https://speedwaysonline.com/
http://www.scrafan.com/

Reader Quiz

1) Where did the first NASCAR Race occur?

2) What is the average speed of a modern race?

3) Who is the winningest driver of all time?

4) What is the weight restriction for Drivers?

5) Do NASCAR drivers need a drivers license?

6) Name one of Bobby's race victories.

7) What 1 sport is more popular than NASCAR?

8) How many sets of tires on avg. are used?

9) What is the nickname of Darlington Raceway?

10) What is Bobby's son's name and nickname?

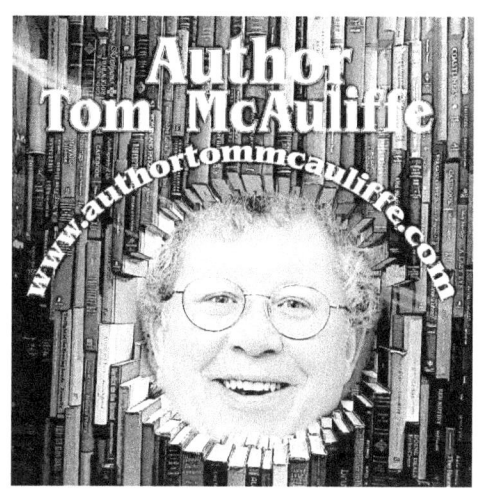

Please Visit:

www.authortommcauliffe.com

Please send questions to:
Bookinfo@nextstopparadise.com

Please Leave a Review!

Member: **Alliance of Independent Authors**

Member: **Emerald Coast Writers**

Books by Author Tom McAuliffe

- **Mr. Mulligan** - *The Life of Champion Armless Golfer Tommy McAuliffe*

- **Nuts!** - *The Life & Times of Gen. Tony McAuliffe*

- **Throttle Up** - *Astronaut Teacher Christa McAuliffe*

- **Mad Dog!** - *Detroit Tiger Dick McAuliffe*

- **Charmed** - *From Motown to Combat & Back*

- **Almost** - *The Road to the Grande*

- **Thunder Road** - *Goodyear, God & Gatorade*

- **Buddy, Brian and Me** - *A Spooky RnR Story*

- **Frozen** - *A WWII Mind Over Matter Tale*

- **Soft Shell** - *Teddy the Talking Turtle*

- **Max and Me** - *Paws Across the Water*

- **Off the Rock** - *Escaping Alcatraz*

Books - eBooks - Audiobooks

On sale at Amazon, Kindle, Audible, Apple Books, Barnes & Noble and your favorite local independent book store!

Also Available at:
WWW.AUTHORTOMMCAULIFFE.COM

MAX AND ME
A Story of Hope
YA
Tom McAuliffe

From the Award Winning Author of 'Mr. Mulligan'
OFF THE ROCK
Escaping Alcatraz
Tom McAuliffe

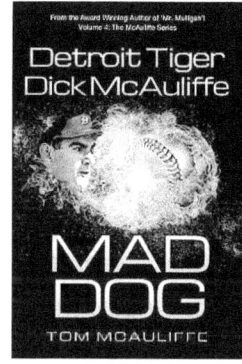

From the Award Winning Author of 'Mr. Mulligan'
Volume 4: The McAuliffe Series
Detroit Tiger Dick McAuliffe
MAD DOG
TOM MCAULIFFE

Buddy Brian and Me
Star Bar
Tom McAuliffe

SOFT SHELL
Teddy the Talking Turtle
YA
Tom McAuliffe

ALMOST
The Road to the Grande
Detroit Bands of the mid-to-Late 60's.
You Almost Remember!
TOM MCAULIFFE

THUNDER ROAD
Goodyear, God & Gatorade!
TOM McAuliffe

FROM THE AWARD WINNING AUTHOR OF "MR. MULLIGAN"...
NUMBER 3 IN "THE MCAULIFFE SERIES"
TEACHER ASTRONAUT CHRISTA MCAULIFFE
THROTTLE UP!
TOM MCAULIFFE

MR. MULLIGAN
The Life of Champion Armless Golfer Tommy McAuliffe
Tom Patrick McAuliffe II

FROZEN
A WWII Mind Over Matter Tale
Tom McAuliffe
From the Award Winning Author of 'Mr. Mulligan'

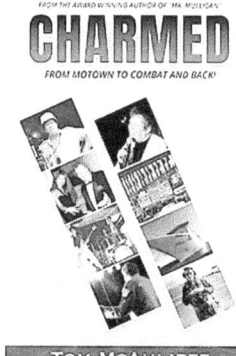

FROM THE AWARD WINNING AUTHOR OF 'MR. MULLIGAN'
CHARMED
FROM MOTOWN TO COMBAT AND BACK!
TOM MCAULIFFE

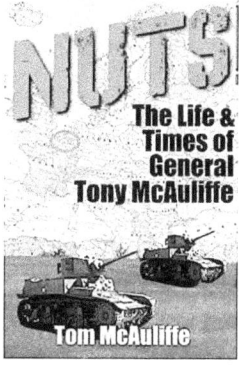

NUTS!
The Life & Times of General Tony McAuliffe
Tom McAuliffe

Reader Quiz
ANSWERS

1) Daytona Beach, Florida

2) 200mph

3) Richard Petty

4) Must weigh more than 200 pounds.

5) No

6) Charlotte 500

7) Football

8) 15 sets of tires

9) The Lady in Black

10) Tommy "Hellcat" Harris

www.ingramcontent.com/pod-product-compliance
Lightning Source LLC
Chambersburg PA
CBHW060425260626
47161CB00005B/1792